實用職場英語教程

主　編　石轉轉
副主編　王夢夢、王慧

崧燁文化

前　言

《實用職場英語教程》是為有一定英語基礎的即將走進職場的高校學生編寫的。本教程旨在指導學生熟悉職場情景、掌握職場中常用的英語對話形式與內容、瞭解職場英語應用文寫作題材與寫作方式，訓練學生的語言信息獲取能力，鞏固學生的英語聽、說、讀、寫、譯能力，提升學生的英語綜合應用能力。本教程選取新穎、實用的案例材料，注重理論與實踐、知識性與趣味性的有效結合，輔以情景式及項目式課后任務，著重培養學生職場英語溝通能力，提高其綜合素質。學生通過學習該課程可達到職場英語中口頭和書面溝通無阻的要求。

本教程由 12 個單元組成，每一單元圍繞一個主題展開，涵蓋了從職業選擇、簡歷、自薦信、面試、公司介紹及名片製作、會議記錄、外貿函電、出差、酒店預訂、宴客、市場行銷及個人理財等職場所涉及的各項內容。

本教程總體設計及編寫大綱由石轉轉、王夢莎完成。第一單元由石轉轉編寫，第二單元由王夢莎編寫，第三單元由羅南英編寫，第四單元由王夢莎、藍珍仔編寫，第五單元由劉雪絨編寫，第六單元由尹蓉、李興玲編寫，第七單元由尹蓉編寫，第八單元由李興玲編寫，第九單元、第十單元由王慧編寫，第十一單元由文婷、鄧豔編寫，第十二單元由文婷、胡庚編寫。另外，初稿的修改與校對工作由王慧和汪瑾完成。

本教程在編寫過程中參閱並借助了各種電子和紙質媒介，書后的參考文獻未能詳盡列出，在此深表感謝。另外，由於編者水平有限，書中難免存在錯漏之處，懇請廣大讀者批評指正。

編　者

CONTENTS

Unit One　Making Your Career Choices ··· (1)

　　Part One　Listening Task ·· (2)

　　Part Two　Speaking Task ·· (3)

　　Part Three　Reading Task ·· (4)

　　Part Four　Supplementary Materials ······································ (8)

　　Part Five　Assignments ·· (9)

Unit Two　Resume ··· (10)

　　Part One　Listening Task ·· (11)

　　Part Two　General Introduction ··· (13)

　　Part Three　Reading Task ·· (14)

　　Part Four　Supplementary Materials ······································ (19)

　　Part Five　Assignment ··· (20)

Unit Three　Application Letters ·· (21)

　　Part One　Listening Task ·· (22)

　　Part Two　General Introduction ··· (23)

　　Part Three　Reading Task ·· (28)

　　Part Four　Supplementary Materials ······································ (32)

Part Five　Assignments ··· (35)

Unit Four　Job Interviews ··· (36)

　　Part One　Listening Task ··· (37)

　　Part Two　General Introduction ··· (38)

　　Part Three　Reading Task ·· (40)

　　Part Four　Supplementary Materials ······································· (44)

　　Part Five　Assignments ·· (45)

Unit 5　Company Introduction & Visiting Cards ························· (47)

　　Part One　Listening Task ··· (48)

　　Part Two　General Introduction ··· (49)

　　Part Three　Reading Task ·· (51)

　　Part Four　Supplementary Materials ······································· (55)

　　Part Five　Assignments ·· (57)

Unit 6　Memos & Minutes ··· (59)

　　Part One　Listening Task ··· (60)

　　Part Two　General Introduction ··· (61)

　　Part Three　Reading Task ·· (65)

　　Part Four　Supplementary Materials ······································· (68)

　　Part Five　Assignment ··· (70)

Unit Seven　Business Correspondence ······································ (71)

　　Part One　Listening Task ··· (72)

　　Part Two　General Introduction ··· (73)

　　Part Three　Reading Task ·· (79)

Part Four	Supplementary Materials	(83)
Part Five	Assignment	(84)

Unit Eight Travel for Business .... (85)

Part One	Listening Task	(86)
Part Two	General Introduction	(87)
Part Three	Reading Task	(89)
Part Four	Supplementary Materials	(93)
Part Five	Assignments	(95)

Unit Nine Making Reservations .... (96)

Part One	Listening Task	(97)
Part Two	Speaking Task	(98)
Part Three	Reading Task	(99)
Part Four	Supplementary Materials	(103)
Part Five	Assignment	(104)

Unit Ten Having Business Dinners .... (106)

Part One	Listening Task	(107)
Part Two	Speaking Task	(108)
Part Three	Reading Task	(109)
Part Four	Supplementary Materials	(113)
Part Five	Assignments	(115)

Unit Eleven Marketing & Sales .... (117)

Part One	Listening Task	(118)
Part Two	Speaking Task	(120)

Part Three　Reading Task ……………………………………………（121）

Part Four　Supplementary Materials ………………………………（125）

Part Five　Assignment …………………………………………………（126）

Unit Twelve　Financial Matters ……………………………………（127）

Part One　Listening Task ……………………………………………（128）

Part Two　Speaking Task ……………………………………………（130）

Part Three　Reading Task ……………………………………………（131）

Part Four　Supplementary Materials ………………………………（135）

Part Five　Assignment …………………………………………………（136）

Appendix：Keys and Tape Scripts …………………………………（137）

Unit One　Making Your Career Choices …………………………（137）

Unit Two　Resume ……………………………………………………（139）

Unit Three　Application Letters ……………………………………（142）

Unit Four　Job Interviews ……………………………………………（144）

Unit Five　Company Introduction & Visiting Cards ……………（148）

Unit Six　Memos & Minutes ………………………………………（150）

Unit Seven　Business Correspondence ……………………………（153）

Unit Eight　Travel for Business ……………………………………（155）

Unit Nine　Making Reservations ……………………………………（157）

Unit Ten　Having Business Dinners ………………………………（161）

Unit Eleven　Marketing & Sales ……………………………………（165）

Unit Twelve　Financial Matters ……………………………………（168）

References ………………………………………………………………（172）

Unit One Making Your Career Choices

Objectives

Students are able to:

- conduct professional personality tests and find job opportunities that best suit themselves;
- read the job advertisements in the newspaper or on the Internet;
- understand daily conversations about making career choices;
- ask for and give suggestions on one's job-hunting.

Part One　Listening Task

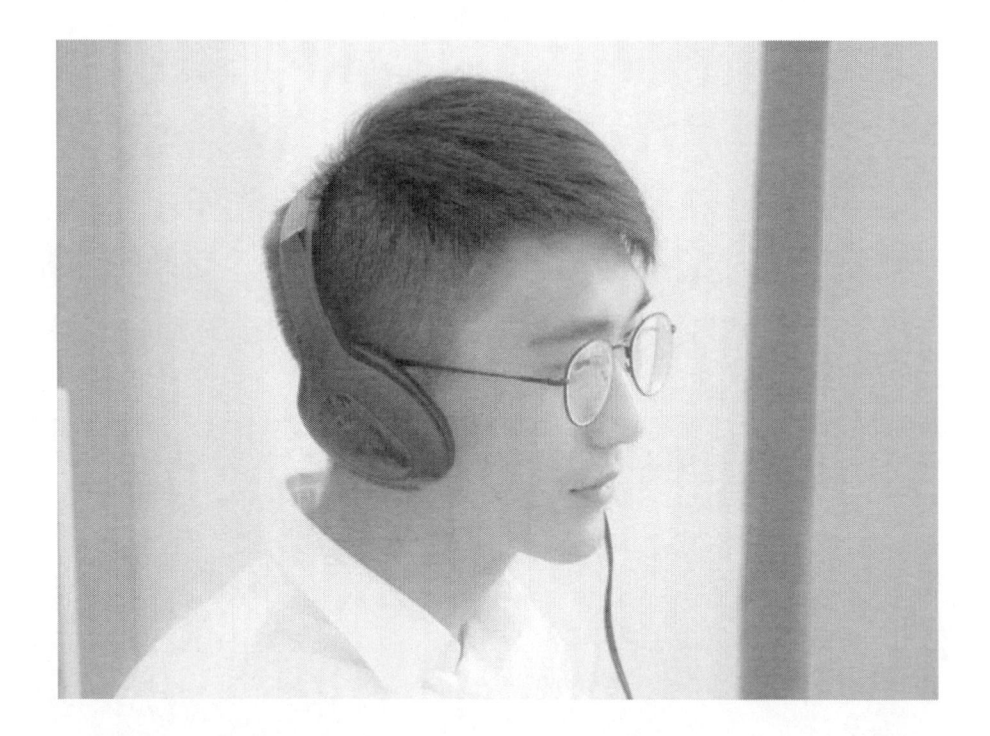

Listen to the dialogue between the two friends and decide whether the following statements are true or false. Write (T) for true and (F) for false.

(　)　1. Consulting with different businesses and finding out what is required in each department are helpful when we are making decisions on the future job.

(　)　2. There are not many career choices for the students who major in Business.

(　)　3. Job hunters should also look at some ads and see what is available in the real world.

(　)　4. When we are making decisions about what we want to do, we can start by thinking about our specific interests in Business.

(　) 5. A job in Human Resources or Management would probably suit John.

(　) 6. We, the job hunters, are supposed to identify our own strengths and weaknesses in each area.

(　) 7. For graduates, it's advisable to visit college counselors.

Part Two　Speaking Task

Brainstorm:

Questions for Discussion

1. Do you have other suggestions to the students who are making their career choices besides what are mentioned in the conversation you've just heard?

2. Which do you think is more important when one chooses a job, high salary or a promising future?

3. What is your ideal job? What have you done to prepare for it?

Part Three Reading Task

Reading Task One

Read the following ads and answer the questions.

Secretary/Receptionist

Required for XA Accounting Firm in city center. Proficiency in MS office, good interpersonal skills, and good telephone manners essential. Candidates should hold a diploma from a recognized business school. Experience an advantage though not a necessity. Apply with resume, copy of diploma and three references.

Accounts Manager

Prestigious language school requires an Internal Accounts Manager to take responsibility for a number of key existing accounts together with the development of new business. Candidates, preferably graduates, with proven ability will report to the Director. Remuneration negotiable and based on qualifications and experience.

Sales Representative

Required for a small but dynamic automobile company. The selected candidate must enjoy all aspects of sales and be willing to research the latest car models. Ability to work in a team and a strong interest in the client are essential. No experience necessary as on-the-job training is provided. Basic salary and commission on car sales.

Questions:

1. What skills are needed for the Secretary/Receptionist position in XA Accounting Firm?

   _____

2. What responsibilities should the Accounts Manager take in the language school?

   _____

3. What does 「remuneration」 mean in the second advertisement?

   _____

4. Is it essential that the Accounts Manager have a university qualification?

   _____

5. What feature of the sales representative job might be a motivating factor?

   _____

Reading Task Two

Read the following passage and choose the right answers.

Understanding the process of making career choices and managing your career is a basic life skill that everyone should understand.

Your career decisions have such a profound effect on all aspects of your life. It's important to have the knowledge and resources needed to make smart, informed decisions. Whether you are looking for a new job, aiming to take the next step at your current job or planning your retirement options, you are making career decisions. Using good resources and the guidance of a career counselor can help you to make those decisions well.

Many people mistakenly believe that choosing a career is a one-time event that happens sometime in early adulthood. However, career management is actually a life-long process, and we continue to make consequential career choices over the years. When people want to take action in their career, career management and job search are about so much more than writing a good resume. If you learn about and act on the following areas of career management, you'll be rewarded throughout your career.

Your interests, abilities, values, personal needs and realities should all be taken into account in any career decision-making process. You spend countless hours at work, and it impacts your life in so many ways; it makes sense that you should be fully informed before making such profound decisions.

Do you know how many different career choices are available to you? Both *The Dictionary of Occupational Titles* (American) and *The National Occupational Classification* (Canadian) list well over 20,000 different job titles. So unless you've actively explored a variety of career options, there's a very good chance that there are great possibilities available to you, and you don't even realize they exist.

Match your understanding of yourself with your understanding of possible career options.

Once you have developed a good understanding of yourself, you will be able to combine that self-knowledge with your career and labor market research to determine potential careers that are a great fit for you.

When you've made a well-informed decision, you're ready to make it happen. Making use of good career guidance and resources will help you to acquire the education, skills, and experience needed to get the job and learn and implement effective job search strategies.

Time spent understanding your needs, researching your career options and developing outstanding job search skills, guided by great career resources, is a powerful investment in your future.

Questions:

1. What's the main idea of the passage?

A) In the process of making career decisions, people should consider interests, abilities, values, personal needs and realities.

B) All the people should have a good knowledge of how to make career choices and manage their career.

C) Career decisions have a great impact on people's life.

D) There are various possibilities available to you of making career decisions.

2. How many tips does the author give on career management?

A) One.　　　B) Two.　　　C) Three.　　　D) Four.

3. It can be inferred that _____.

A) Career decision is misunderstood by many people because they don't take it as a lifelong process.

B) Your career will be definitely successful if you make a well-informed decision.

C) Making yourself understood can help you make a final choice.

D) Writing a good resume can help you find a good job.

4. Which of the following statements is NOT TRUE according to the passage?

A) Your interests in the occupation you choose are vital.

B) Good career guidance and resources can help you gain the skills and experience.

C) You are to make significant decisions without good resources and the guidance of a career adviser.

D) Planning your retirement options is related to career management.

Part Four Supplementary Materials

Useful Expressions: Occupations

general manager	總經理	cashier	出納員
CEO（Chief Executive Officer）	總裁	PR/HR/ sales manager	公關部/人力資源部/銷售部經理
controller	財務主管	senior auditor	高級審計師
senior accountant	高級會計師	accounting assistant	會計助理
CPA（Certified Public Accountant）	註冊會計師	bond analyst	證券分析師
administrative assistant	行政助理	marketing representative	銷售代表
general auditor	審計長	purchaser	採購員
broker	經紀人	auditing clerk	審計員
storekeeper	倉庫管理員	architect	建築師
mechanic	機械師	quality inspector	質檢員
bond trader	證券交易員	legal adviser	法律顧問
real estate staff	房地產職員	operational manager	業務經理
insurance actuary	保險公司理賠員	civil engineer	土木工程師

Useful Sentences: Asking for & Giving Advice

---

1. What's your suggestion/advice?

2. Don't you think we should start job-hunting?

3. Shall we ask the college counselor for advice?

4. Why don't we log on the Internet and do some professional personality tests?

5. Why don't you call your parents?

6. Why not find out about available jobs?

7. Have you thought about being a teacher?

8. You'd better read the advertisements in the local newspaper and try to find a job that matches your skills, qualifications, and interests.

9. How about/What about setting up your own business?

10. If I were you, I'd consider the salary first.

Part Five Assignments

1. Ask your parents, teachers or friends for advice on your career planning and make decisions.
2. Finish the personality tests recommended in the class.

Unit Two　Resume

Objectives

Students are able to:

- know the importance of a resume;
- understand the definitions of「resume」and「basic resume」;
- be familiar with the essential elements of a basic resume;
- acquire some useful expressions in writing a resume;
- complete an effective resume.

Part One Listening Task

Listening Task One

Listen to a Human Resources manager talking about what to include in a resume and tick (√) the points that are mentioned and cross (×) the points that are not mentioned.

( ) address   ( ) experience
( ) age   ( ) interests
( ) all your education ( ) marital status
( ) consenting references ( ) religion
( ) e-mail   ( ) volunteer work

Listening Task Two

Listen to two people from the Human Resources Department discussing the two applicants and fill in blanks in the following exercise.

Jane was (1) _____ by both Applicant 1 and Applicant 2 for different reasons. Applicant 1 has quite a lot of experience – over (2) _____, but he is a little short in (3) _____ qualifications. Applicant 2 has an M.A. in HR as well as a General Business degree, but on the experience side she is a little (4) _____. However, Applicant 1 has had wide range of (5) _____ in very important HR areas at (6) _____ levels. As the company is looking for someone who's a (7) _____ and that's probably easier for a person who's (8) _____ in the (9) _____. Both applicants will be (10) _____ for an interview.

Part Two General Introduction

1. **The importance of a resume:**

    A resume is an important tool in careering as it helps make an initial impression on the potential employers.

2. **The definition of 「resume」 and 「basic resume」:**

    A *resume* or *C.V.* is a short written account of one's education and previous jobs that one sends to an employer when looking for a new job.

    A *basic resume* needs the applicant to write down his or her basic information such as education experience as well as general personal information.

3. **A basic resume includes:**

    ✓ Educational background information (usually writing from the high school level which includes degree, major, university, department, date, main courses, special electives);

    ✓ Your professional skills (the skills about your major and the position that you want to be employed);

    ✓ Honors and awards (usually writing from the awards that you acquire in the college. The lowest one should be at the high school level);

    ✓ Certificates (The level should be as the same as that of honors and awards);

    ✓ Work experience if you have any.

4. **Tips on writing an effective resume:**

    ✓ Do not use any templates;

- ✓ Be professional and concise;
- ✓ Be honest;
- ✓ Do not exaggerate;
- ✓ Enhance your advantages and avoid disadvantages;
- ✓ Do not mention politics unless your are required to;
- ✓ Write down the formal, practical and relevant work experience;
- ✓ Refine your language but do not use abbreviations;
- ✓ Learn to use bullet points;
- ✓ Always begin with a verb;
- ✓ Do not always write 「I」 in your resume.

Part Three Reading Task

Reading Task One

Read through the following resume sample and answer the question.

Xi Yuan

Residency: Chongqing

Cell: 18535678901

E-mail: yuan.xi@live.cn

Job Objective: To apply for a position in English teaching in a college/university.

Education

08/2010-03/2012	Department & University: The School of Arts and Humanities, Swansea University, UK
	Academic Degree: Master of Arts
	Major: Teaching English as a Foreign Language
	Main courses: Vocabulary Teaching and Learning, Communicative Language Teaching, Discourse Analysis for ELT, Computer-assisted Language Learning, Classroom Teaching Practice.
09/2006-06/2010	Department & University: The School of Foreign Languages, Chongqing Normal University, China
	Academic Degree: Bachelor of Arts
	Major: Educational English

Professional Skills

✓ Good English capability in terms of listening, speaking, reading and writing;

✓ Solid theoretical foundation and practice knowledge of English Education;

✓ Mastery of the methods of teaching English as a foreign language;

✓ Classroom teaching experience;

✓ Accumulation for innovative thoughts on English teaching methods;

✓ Mastery of Microsoft Word, Microsoft PowerPoint, etc.

Honors and Certificates

2011　Honor of Swansea University International Scholarship;

2010　IELTS Test (International English Language Testing System): 7 points;

2010　Teaching Certificate (teaching subject: English);

2009　Honor of First Prize Scholarship, Chongqing Normal University;

2009　Occupational Qualification Certificate of Psychological Consultant, the People's Republic of China;

2009　Certificate of Standard Chinese Proficiency Test (2nd grade, A level);

2008　Certificate of TEM-8.

Question:

What qualifications do you think a good English teacher should have?

_____

_____

_____

_____

Reading Task Two

Read the following passage and answer the questions.

Should your education be proudly at the top of the C. V. or among the optional sections at the end? It all depends on who you are and what job you are trying to get. If you have just left school, college or university, your education experience is going to be more immediately relevant and should therefore be prominently displayed early on. Your potential employer may be keen to hire recent graduates and will wish to see exactly what your educational attainments are. This means you can give plenty of details of curricula, theses and grades. However, if you have been in the world of work for 20 years, your education is of little interest to an employer and should go in skeletal form near the bottom of the C. V. What you have achieved since leaving full-time education is obviously more indicative of your value.

Another thing to bear in mind is that higher qualifications imply lower ones. If you have only got GCSEs, fine. If, however, you have a bachelor's degree, it is unnecessary to mention your GCSEs, or even your A-levels, unless they are spectacularly good. A recruiter will simply assume they were taken at the usual time and is unlikely to be interested in how many there were and what grades they were. The same applies to a Master's degree or Ph. D. The higher qualification makes the mention of any lower ones redundant.

If you feel you need to mention more in the way of academic attainments, for example, as a recent graduate or as someone with professional qualifications or other postgraduate training, the section should be organized in reverse chronological order, like your work experience section.

Finally, the education section can be the place to mention the all-important computer skills that continue to dominate working life. Different jobs and professions will require you to have an understanding of different computer packages, and if you have good working knowledge of these, it is worth mentioning that you know they exist, or have been trained to use them. If you are applying for a job more closely related to IT, your technical proficiencies should have a relevant section of their own (entitled 「computer efficiency」 or 「computer skills」 or 「technical expertise」) much higher up the priority list.

Questions:

1. Why should recent graduates put the education section near the top of their C. V.?

　_____

2. What term does the author use to mean just the main piece of information, nothing more?

　_____

3. Under what two circumstances would you include your A-level results in a C. V.?

　_____

4. What qualifications should you mention first?

　_____

5. What should you do if you're searching for employment in the IT field?

　_____

Part Four Supplementary Materials

Useful Expressions: Departments & Majors

Department of Finance	金融系	Department of Management Engineering	管理工程系
Finance	金融學	Property Management	物業管理
Insurance	保險學	Land Resources Management	土地資源管理
Investment	投資學	Real Estate Management	房地產經營與管理
Motor Insurance	汽車保險	Engineering Management	工程管理
Credit Management	信用管理	City Management	城市管理
Department of Accounting	會計系	Department of Economics	經濟系
Accounting	會計學	Trade Economy	貿易經濟
Financial Management	財務管理	Economics	經濟學
Asset Assessment	資產評估	Economic Statistics	經濟統計學
Auditing	審計學	Internet and New Media	網路與新媒體
Department of Commerce	商務系	Department of Information Engineering	信息工程系
International Economy and Trade	國際經濟與貿易	Logistics Management	物流管理
Exhibition Economy and Management	會展經濟與管理	Electronic Commerce	電子商務
International Business	國際商務	Industrial Engineering	工業工程
		Information Management and Information System	信息管理與信息系統

Useful Sentences: Stating Job Objectives

1. A responsible administrative position which will provide challenges and freedom where I can bring my initiative and creativity into full play.

2. An executive assistant position utilizing interests, training and experience in office administration.

3. An entry-level position in sales. Eventual goal: Manager of sales department.

4. A position in foreign trade department, with opportunities for advancement to management position in the department.

5. To begin as an accounting trainee and eventually become a manager.

6. An entry-level position in an accounting environment, which ultimately leads to financial management.

7. A position as data-processing manager that will enable me to use my knowledge of computer systems.

8. A position requiring analytical skills in the financial or investment field.

9. A position as a computer programmer in a medium-sized firm.

10. To serve as sales promoter in a multinational corporation with a view to promotion in position and assignment in parent company's branch abroad.

Part Five Assignment

Please prepare a basic resume for your future job and share it with the whole class.

Unit Three   Application Letters

Objectives

Students are able to:

- understand what an application letter is;
- read an application letter;
- grasp the features and essential elements of an application letter;
- acquire some useful expressions in writing an application letter;
- complete an effective application letter.

Part One Listening Task

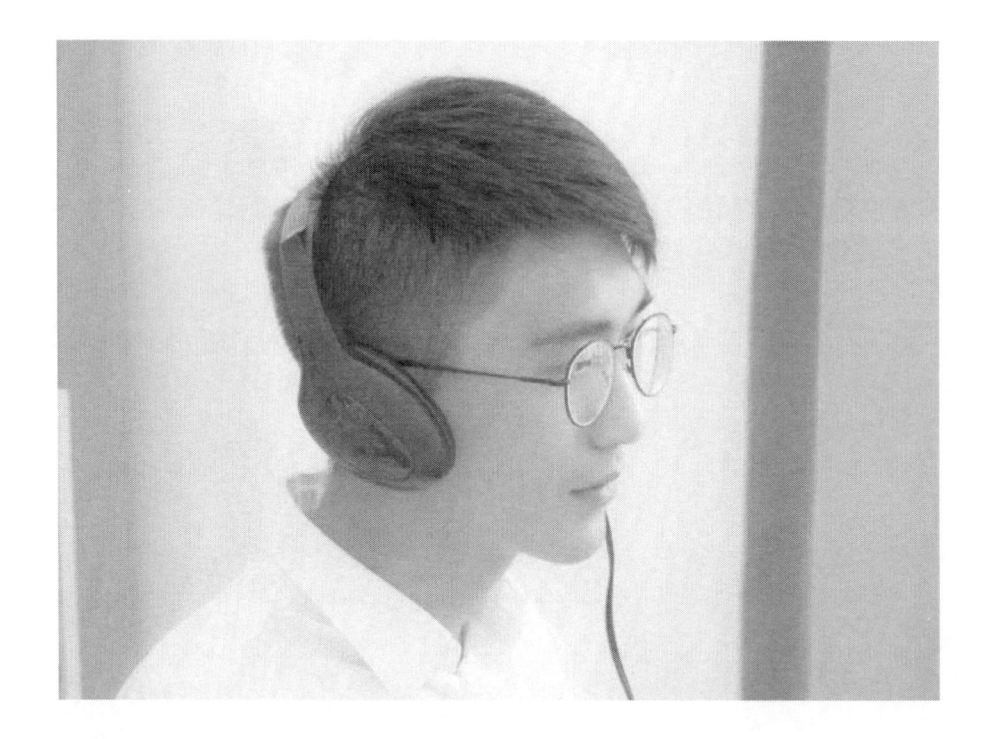

Listen to Martha and John talking about their strengths and weaknesses and finish the following exercises. Complete the blanks with the information you hear.

John: John is really good at (1) _____ and has a way with people that would be very good in sales and (2) _____. As for the weaknesses, he is a bit (3) _____ about getting himself moving. But it's not a good idea to tell a (4) _____ employer that he is lazy, so he is advised to say he is considered a bit (5) _____, and he is working on his organizational skills.

Martha: Martha's skills are (6) _____. She is good at planning and seeing things (7) _____. Some people would say that she is (8) _____, but this may be because she has a lot of drive and (9) _____ to get the job done. She can organize herself and (10) _____ everything as she goes along.

Part Two General Introduction

1. The definition of an application letter:

An application letter (cover letter) is also called *a self-recommendation letter*. Applicants or job-hunters write this letter to employers to make them know about their skills, trust their abilities and give them an opportunity. It is a letter that individuals write and send to their ideal companies or organizations in order to get a position. It needs to be concise and clear.

2. How to write an application letter:

An application letter consists of one's motivation, self-introduction, personal skills, the ending and attachment. The principal parts are: the heading, date line, inside address, salutation, body, complimentary closing, and signature line. In addition to these basic components, there are several other elements that may be added to the letter depending upon its contents: A subject line, announcing the purpose of the letter, precedes the salutation.

3. The importance of an application letter:

It is the first thing an employer sees, so it's often the first impression you will make!

4. Tips on writing an effective application letter:

✓ Customize the application letter for the particular job;

✓ Indicate your purposes or reasons clearly;

✓ Give accurate and objective personal information;

✓ Emphasize what you have to contribute to the company or organization;

✓ In bold type, highlight your skills that match the job description;

✓ Use polite words, and expose yourself confidently and optimistically;

✓ Fix ALL spelling errors and typos;

✓ Personalize your application letter. If possible, address your application letter to the person in charge of interviewing and hiring.

Notes:

Your application letter should be clear, concise, correct, courteous, objective, relevant and confident.

5. Sample study:

Sample I

A Letter of Application for an Assistant

Dear Sir/Madam,

　　I wish to apply for the position for a part-time assistant you advertised in *Zhejiang Daily* during the coming summer vacation.

　　I am a student of Zhejiang University, which is only five minutes walk from your shop. I feel that my qualifications and work experience make me a suitable candidate for the job, which, according to the advertisement, demands a multi-lingual person with some experience. Chinese is my mother tongue, and I have a fair mastery of English. As a keen traveler, I have learned some Japanese and French, and have acquired an understanding of the cultures of Japan and France. As for experience, I worked part time as a waiter in a pizza hut. Therefore, I am confident that you will find my service satisfactory.

　　I hope you will take my application into consideration favorably and entitle me to an interview at your convenience. I can be reached at 0573-8836254.

　　Thank you for considering my application again. I am looking forward to your reply and, eventually, meeting you.

Yours sincerely,
John Gordon

Sample II

A Letter of Application for a Salesman

Dear Sir,

    I believe that my sales background fits me for the position you advertised in Thursday's newspaper, so I ask that you consider my qualification. I graduated from Chongqing University in July 2010. My experience has included two years as salesman in the Men's Clothing Department for Yishion; and three years in the Men's Shop for G2000, where I am still employed. My reason for wishing to make a change at this time is that there seems no opportunity for advancement in my present position, and I feel that my ability and training, as well as my interest in my work, should lead to advancement and a higher salary.

    I am enclosing my resume together with my photo, and believe that they may be found satisfactory. I assure you that if appointed, I will do my best to give you satisfaction. If you agree with me, please write a letter to me or phone me. I live at No. 1 Renmin Road, Chongqing. My telephone number is 13654371289.

Yours sincerely,
Zhang Lin

Sample III

A letter of Application for a Graduate Program

Dear Mr. Elizabeth Williams,

  I am a student in the Department of Physics of Chongqing University, expecting to graduate with a bachelor's degree in July next year. I am very much interested in pursuing a Master's degree in Particle Physics at the Particle Physics Department of Oxford University. From my review of graduate programs and discussion with my professors, I find that Oxford University has the largest particle physics group in the UK, with a large academic and support staff. I intend to enter in the autumn of 2016. In my undergraduate years, I have worked hard. As you can see from my curriculum vitae, my GPA in major courses is 3.8/4.0 and I have remained top 5% of about 100 students.

  I have also worked with Dr. Liu Wei and Professor Luo Lei on research topics like the applied physics at the enterprise level. Because of my excellence in study and research, I have been awarded scholarships three times. In addition, I am well-prepared linguistically to further my studies in the UK. My IELTS score is 7.5 and my GRE score is 160+166+4.

  I would be grateful if you would send me the application forms for admission and financial support at your earliest convenience. Thank you for your consideration. I look forward to hearing from you soon.

Yours sincerely,
Lin Pengpeng

6. Format of application letters for a graduate program:

Room 205, 34 Dingxi Road　　　　　　　　　　　　　　　（申請人地址）

Changning District

Shanghai, 200002

PRC

December 11, 2015　　　　　　　　　　　　　　　　　　（申請日期）

Judy Williams, Admission Administrator

Graduate School Admissions　　　　　　　　　　　　　（信內被申請學校地址）

Michigan State University

East Lansing, MI 48824

Dear Mrs. Williams,　　　　　　　　　　　　　　　　　　（稱呼）

　　I wish to apply for admission to Education Psychology at Michigan State University to pursue a Master's degree and further a Doctor's degree in Education. My intended time of admission is the July of 2016. (申請專業與學位、擬入學時間)

　　If possible, I also wish to obtain graduate assistantship so that I may support myself and obtain some experience while pursuing my graduate studies. (申請獎學金)

　　In 2009 I got my B. A. degree in English Language and Literature from Guangzhou Institute of Foreign Languages. In the past six years, I've been employed as a teacher at Guangzhou University. (教育背景、工作經歷)

　　Would you please send me the application forms for admission and financial support at your earliest convenience? Thank your very much. (索要申請表格)

　　　　　　　　　　　　　　　　　　　　　　　　　　Yours sincerely,

　　　　　　　　　　　　　　　　　　　　　　　　　　Dong Min

Part Three Reading Task

Reading Task One

Read the following passage and answer the questions.

How to Write an Application Letter

  Writing a letter is a common practice if you wish to make a request or ask for a favor. Whether we avail a service or assistance, apply for a job, leave, loan, and admission, we convey the message via a letter. This letter is called an application letter. It is a written request that is drafted to inform the addressee what you expect them to do.

  The content of the application letter depends on the type of request made. The tone used in the letter is polite. The main purpose of the letter is focused in the very first paragraph, so that the reader can understand what the letter is about in the first glance.

The main body of the letter will give all the essential facts and information to the concerned authority. If it is a job application letter, you have to explain how you will help the organization to develop if they hire you. An application for a leave will mention the reason you need it. Similarly, a loan application must display for what purpose you are asking the loan and how you have planned to repay it.

Here are some tips that will help you in drafting a letter of application:

The letter has to start with the sender's name and address. This has to be followed with a receiver's name and address. Date has to be inserted in between the two addresses in a standard format (month/date/year). All these things have to be aligned to the left side.

The letter of application has to have a salutation in the form of a word「Dear」followed by the name of addressee. Then you can begin with the main body of the letter.

In the first paragraph, write the purpose of sending the letter along with some references. The letter content depends upon the nature of the content. For example, if you are applying for a job, mention how you learned about the job opportunity and which position you are applying for. If you are seeking an admission, then mention the name of the course you wish to pursue and the reason for choosing the same university. If you are applying for a leave, write the period of leave you wish to take and the reason for the same in a few words.

The second paragraph talks about additional details you wish to convey to the reader. For example, in case of a job application letter, give a brief introduction of your career profile. For admissions application letter, talk about the qualifications previously acquired and your future plans. In case of a leave application letter, give a detailed perspective of the reason for your leave and the importance of the situation. You must also state when you will resume the office.

Be certain that the letter possess strong convincing abilities. Since this is an application letter, it is obvious that you are making a request for something. There is an absolute possibility that several others may have sent similar applications. Hence, equip your letter with many positive points and reasoning to convince the reader as to why you deserve the favor.

The letter should focus on how unique you are and why you should be selected for the interview or admission.

End the letter on a positive note. Close the letter with a phrase like thanking you, yours truly, sincerely yours, etc. The complimentary closure should be followed by your name and signature. If this is an official letter, write your designation. Alternatively, if it is an academic letter, write your class and division.

Print the letter on good-quality paper. A good-quality paper is super white, crisp, and of A4 size.

Use professional fonts like Times New Roman, Arial, and a font size that is readable.

The letter has to be flawless. Proofread the letter thoroughly before dispatching it. Make sure the letter is factually and grammatically accurate.

An application letter must be effective in its presentation. Since the letter aims at fulfilling some purpose, it must be convincing and impressive enough to help you achieve what you desire.

Questions:

1. What tone should be used in an application letter?

_____

2. What should a loan application display?

_____

3. What should you include in the letter if you are applying for a leave?

_____

4. How can you close an application letter?

_____

5. What does a 「good-quality」 paper mean?

_____

Reading Task Two

Read the following passage and choose the right answers.

The purpose of a letter of application is to help you to 「sell」 yourself. You should state the job you want clearly, and should tell what your abilities are and what you have done. It should be simple, human, personal and brief without leaving out any necessary facts.

In writing a letter of application, a possible employer may want to know a number of important things. What are your qualifications? What achievements have you made? And what are your aims? The opening paragraph is perhaps the important part. Try to keep your opening sentences to the needs or interests of the employer, not to your own needs or desires.

Be clear about the kind of job for which you are now applying. College graduates looking for their first positions often ask 「What can I provide in a letter?」 Employers want to know about your experience. Certainly, a beginner has no experience. The answer is that everything you have ever done is experience.

It is important to write good strong closing words for your letter. Ask for an interview or give the possible employer something definite to do or expect. An excellent idea is to enclose an envelope with your address and a stamp. That makes it easier for a possible employer to get in touch with you.

Questions:

    1. The purpose of writing a letter of application is to _____.

    A) sell a product to somebody else   B) try your best to get a good job

    C) help a company to hire people   D) make others know about you

    2. What can be the most important thing in writing an application letter? _____.

A) The abilities you have obtained   B) The kind of job you like

C) The first paragraph of the letter   D) The experience you have had

3. A possible employer may want to know about _____.

A) your personal life   B) your hopes for the future

C) your future colleagues   D) your family life

4. College graduates who are looking for their first positions usually have no _____.

A) desires in salary   B) definite purposes

C) experience in working   D) ability to handle the job

5. For the convenience of a possible employer to contact you, you'd better enclose _____.

A) a recent photo of you

B) some money in the letter

C) an application form for the job

D) an envelope with your address and stamp on

Part Four Supplementary Materials

Useful Expressions

1. The beginning sentence of an application letter

① I would like to apply for the job you are offering in today's *China Daily*/admission to your college.

② With reference to your advertisement in *Yancheng Evening News* of May 16th for an accountant, I offer myself for the post.

③ Your advertisement for a sales manager in the *Guangzhou Daily* of August 10th has interested me very much. I feel I can fill that vacancy.

④ I wish to be considered for the position of Personnel Manager advertised in today's newspaper.

2. Describing one's education

① I am now studying at Sichuan International Studies University and will soon be graduated as an English major.

② I am a graduate student in the Physics Department of Beijing University. I am majoring in Solar Physics.

③ I specialized in Nuclear and High Energy Physics at the University of Science and Technology of China, from which I graduated in July 2014 with highest honors.

3. Describing one's experiences

① For the past three years, I have been in the office of the Star Trading Company, where I have been an accountant.

② At the university I majored in International Secretary, and did two years' part-time job in a foreign trade company.

③ My experience at ABC Company has been both educational and rewarding.

④ Since my graduation from Guangzhou Institute of Foreign Trade five years ago, I have been employed as a sales representative at the Chaozhou Garment Factory.

4. Describing one's personal abilities

① I am able to take dictation in English and translate it rapidly into Chinese.

② I am a dedicated professional with skills and experience necessary for a secretary.

③ Being well acquainted with office work, I could make myself generally useful, should there be an opportunity of serving in your company.

5. Describing the reasons of one's quitting the previous job

① While I'm quite happy in my present work, I hope to enter a company where there are more opportunities for advancement.

② I find it absolutely necessary to seek an employment which can enable me to earn a higher salary to cope with the growing high cost of living.

③ I am desirous of leaving this employment in order to improve myself and have more responsibilities.

6. Asking for an interview or consideration

① I should be pleased to attend for an interview at your convenience, when I could give you further details concerning myself.

② I hope that you will grant me for an interview at your earliest convenience.

③ If you are interested in my application, I would be glad to come for an interview. Thank you for your consideration.

④ If you need detailed information regarding my working experience, I shall be happy to provide upon request.

7. Asking for reply

① Your prompt response will be much appreciated.

② I am looking forward to hearing from you soon.

8. Asking for application forms

① I would appreciate it if you could send me the application forms for admission and financial aid.

② Could you send me more information on your department and an application form for admission?

③ I am writing this letter to request application materials for graduate admission and financial support.

④ Would you please send me the necessary materials at your convenience?

9. Enclosure

① I am enclosing my curriculum vitae together with my photographs.

② Enclosed please find a resume, a photocopy of my academic degree certificate, and two photographs.

③ You will find enclosed a photocopy of my ID card, a photocopy of my university diploma, and a photocopy of my technical qualification certificate.

10. Describing one's economic status

① Our government will provide me with all living expenses.

② I have sufficient financial resources to cover my educational expenses. So, I shall not seek financial support in any form from your institute.

③ If possible, I wish to obtain a graduate assistantship so that I may support myself and obtain some teaching experience while pursuing graduate studies.

Part Five Assignments

1. Write an application letter according to the outline given below in Chinese. You should write down at least 120 words.

    假設你叫林然，從報上得知某公司欲招聘一名英語翻譯。你的個人資料如下：

    ➢ 簡況：

    姓名：林然；年齡：29歲；身高：1.60米；健康狀況：良好；業餘愛好：游泳、唱歌、跳舞。

    ➢ 簡歷：1996年重慶大學畢業後分配到巴蜀中學工作，1998年調至重慶一中工作至今。

    ➢ 工作：工作認真負責，與人相處融洽。

    ➢ 特長：精通英語，尤其口語，已將多本中文書籍譯成英語，懂一些日語、能用日語與外賓對話。

    ➢ 聯繫電話：18523749888。

    ➢ 聯繫地址：重慶市人民路二號。

2. Suppose you are an undergraduate who will graduate next year. Write an application letter to a company asking for a job which is related to your major.

Unit Four Job Interviews

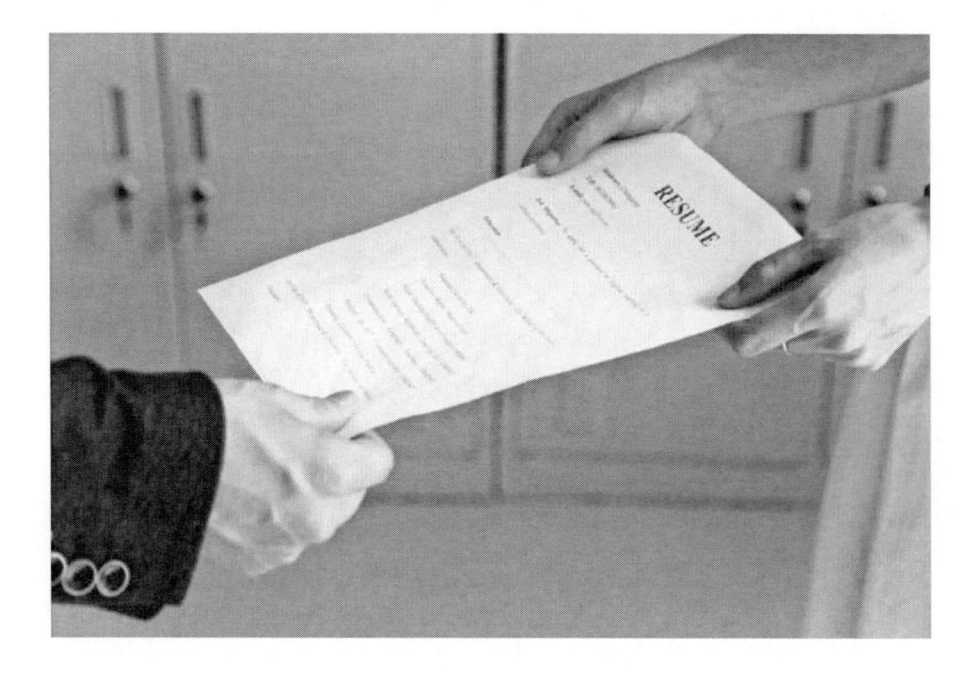

Objectives

Students are able to:

- understand what an interview is and how to be a good interviewee;
- know how to prepare for and behave well in an interview;
- acquire some useful expressions in doing an interview;
- go through an interview smoothly.

Unit Four Job Interviews 37

Part One Listening Task

Listening Task One

Please watch Video 1 and try to find out the advantages of the applicant.

Possible answers:

_____

_____

_____

Listening Task Two

Please watch Video 2 and find out the tips to ace a job interview.

Possible answers:

Part Two General Introduction

1. What is a job interview?

A job interview is a formal meeting between employers and applicants. It is a very effective way for the interviewer to know better about applicants. To learn how to behave properly in the interview is very important for the applicants, because an interview is always the best chance for them to show their merits.

2. How to leave a good impression on your potential employer:

✓ Be yourself. Too much is as bad as too little. We should show our good qualities in a natural way.

✓ Use your eyes. If you lose proper eye contact, you are at risk of losing the happiness of your whole life.

✓ Lighten up. To make others comfortable, you have to appear comfortable yourself.

3. Tips on how to behave well in an interview:

✓ Clothes and grooming: formal, neat, clean, suitable for the interview;

✓ Posture: proper body control and eye contact;

✓ Language: polite and appropriate; careful listening and appropriate responses to questions;

✓ Manners and breeding: polite and adult behavior;

✓ Preparation: well-informed about the company and the job requirement;

✓ Motivation: the degree to which the applicant really longs for the job;

✓ Attitude toward oneself: The applicant should be modest but be willing to mention his / her advantages and admit disadvantages;

✓ Potential: the degree to which the applicant is likely to succeed in the job if hired.

Part Three　Reading Task

Reading Task One

Read the following interview and choose the right answers.

In an Interview

(Cindy is in the interview now. She graduated from college this year and now she is applying for the position of secretary. Alan is the manager of XZA Company, a multinational accounting firm. He is interviewing Cindy.)

Alan: Good morning. Welcome to our company.

Cindy: Good morning.

Alan: Hello, Cindy. I'm Alan. I'm the manager of this company. I noticed that you had many courses in your college. Which subject is your favorite?

Cindy: Management Consultancy, because it's very special for my major. I learned not only consultancy, but also managing.

Alan: Good. You mentioned in your resume that you worked as an assistant in YAB Company for a month. What did you do there?

Cindy: I made some financial status analysis and forecasting and made the financial budget. I tried my best to get familiar with the whole function of the department.

Alan: Did you work overtime?

Cindy: Yes. Sometimes, but not very often.

Alan: OK. How did you feel?

Cindy: I could find fun from work.

Alan: I see. My next question is what you know about our company?

Cindy: I know you are a very big multinational professional company and have branches around the world, about 159 offices in this country.

Alan: Yes! Accurate!

Cindy: And you have very big clients.

Alan: I think you know us a lot. So that's all my questions for you. Do you have any questions for us?

Cindy: Yes. What kind of training can you provide to all the employees?

Alan: That's a very good question. We have training programs for all levels of staff. And we also have some e-learning programs. You'll have a chance.

Cindy: That would be very wonderful.

Alan: Yes. That's the benefit you can get. And thank you for your interest in our company. You'll be informed in a week.

Cindy: OK. Thank you very much.

Questions:

1. What is Cindy's attitude towards overtime work?

A) She feels angry about it.

B) She feels bored about it.

C) She feels pleased to do it.

D) She learns a lot from it.

2. What can we infer about Cindy from the interview?

A) She worked hard when she was in YAB Company.

B) She is majoring in Financial Management.

C) She is inexperienced in financial analysis.

D) She cares a lot about the salary.

3. Which statement is incorrect according to the conversation?

A) XZA Company provides the staff with training programs.

B) XZA is a domestic corporation.

C) Cindy tried to get some information about XZA Company before the interview.

D) Cindy is interested in Management Consultancy.

Reading Task Two

Read the following interview and answer the questions.

Changing a Job

(Cindy is an applicant. After 3 years' working in XZA Company, she would like to change a job now. Mark is the personnel manager.)

Mark: Good morning! Take your seat, please.

Cindy: Good morning!

Mark: I'm the personnel manager, and I received your letter yesterday. You are one of the applicants for the manager assistant.

Cindy: Yes, sir.

Mark: You said that you worked as a staff in XZA Company for three years. What did you do?

Cindy: Yes, I worked in an executive branch as a secretary.

Mark: So, why would you like to change the job?

Cindy: I am hoping to get an offer of a better position. If opportunity knocks, I will take it.

Mark: I see. According to your C.V., you are just the person we need. How long would you like to stay with this company?

Cindy: I will stay as long as I can continue to learn and to grow in my field.

Mark: OK. I got it. That's all I need to know. Do you have any questions for us?

Cindy: Thank you, sir. Could I ask about the salary?

Mark: The starting salary is not high, but the fringe benefits are much more. If you do well, we will give you raises in a short time.

Cindy: I see.

Mark: OK. That's all for the interview. We will contact you in three days.

Cindy: Thank you very much. I'm looking forward to hearing from you.

Questions:

1. What's the relationship between Cindy and Mark?

_____

2. What did Cindy do in XZA Company?

_____

3. Why did Cindy want to change her job?

   _____

4. How long would Cindy like to stay with Mark's company?

   _____

5. How is the salary if Cindy works in Mark's company?

   _____

Part Four Supplementary Materials

Useful Expressions: Personality

generous	慷慨的	humorous	幽默的
kind-hearted	熱心的	loyal	忠心的
modest	謙虛的	optimistic	樂觀的
outgoing	外向的	patient	有耐心的
sincere	真誠的	talented	有才干的
cooperative	有合作精神的	independent	獨立的
aggressive	有進取心的	ambitious	有雄心壯志的
competent	能勝任的	steady	踏實的
expressive	善於表達的	industrious	勤奮的
ingenious	有獨創性的	analytical	善於分析的
intelligent	理解力強的	sensible	明白事理的
precise	一絲不苟的	adaptable	適應力強的

Useful Sentences: Questions Usually Asked by the Interviewers

1. Tell me something about yourself.
2. Have you had any work experience?
3. Do you have any related certificates?
4. What did you do in your practice job?
5. What appeals to you about working in our company?
6. What are your particular strengths and weaknesses?
7. Do you work well under stress or pressure?
8. What are your future plans?
9. What are your particular language and computer skills?
10. Describe your greatest achievement in the past.

Part Five Assignments

1. **Each student prepares a self-introduction according to the following hints. You are required to report to the whole class.**

    Hints: Describe yourself.

    Personal details that need to be included:

    ➢ Name, age and character;

    ➢ Education background from senior high school;

    ➢ College (e.g. name of college, major, courses, etc.);

    ➢ Work experience including part-time jobs;

    ➢ Your hobbies.

2. **Mock interview.** Students work in pairs or groups to make a mock interview after class. Performance in class will be preferred.

Unit 5　Company Introduction & Visiting Cards

Objectives

Students are able to:

- understand a company introduction and get the major facts;
- make a company introduction after learning some useful sentences;
- learn the basic information and layout of visiting cards;
- design a visiting card for themselves.

Part One Listening Task

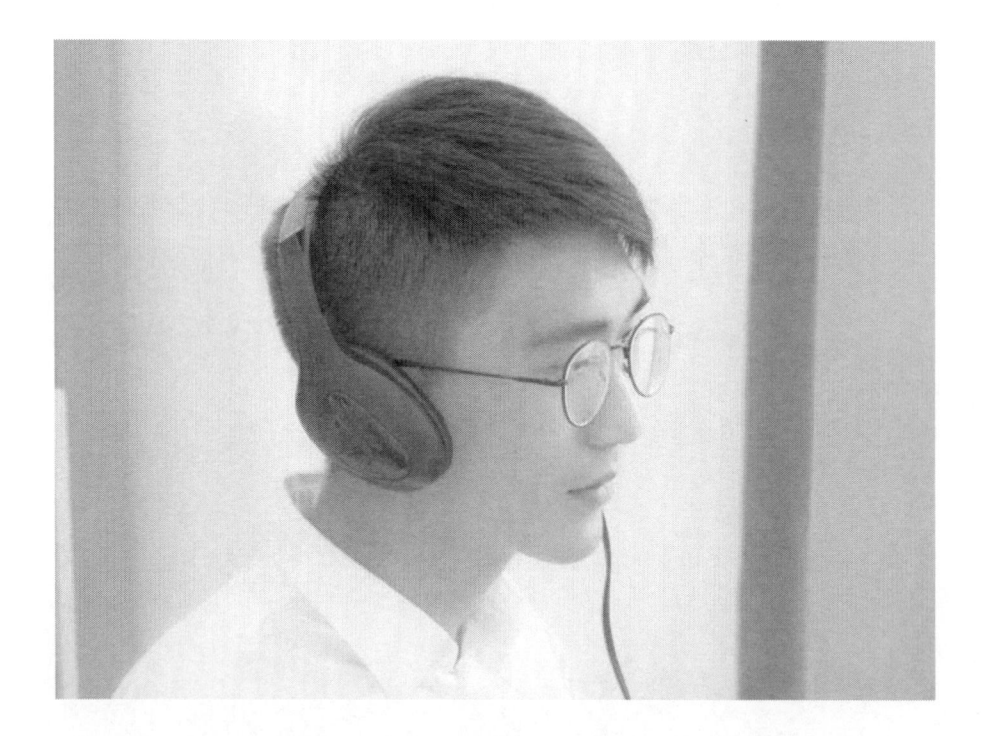

Listen to the dialogue and decide whether the following statements are true or false. Write (T) for true and (F) for false.

(　) 1. The company was owned by the state.

(　) 2. Their registered capital was 5 million *yuan* in 1983.

(　) 3. They import and export commodities popular in the global market.

(　) 4. Their olive oil is imported from European countries.

(　) 5. More than half of their employees have a Master's degree or above.

Part Two General Introduction

1. The function of「company introduction」:

A company introduction gives potential customers an overview of who you are and what you do. It is also a major contributor towards the first impression customers will have on your company and is a great opportunity to gain their trust. A company introduction usually includes the year in which the company was established, the company's location, what products or service the company offers, any foreign investment the company may have, how orders are handled, quality control procedures and number of staff, etc.

2. How to make a company introduction:

1) The type of corporation:

✓ Our corporation is a large state-owned enterprise.

✓ We deal with the import and export of commodities popular in the international market.

✓ Our line of business is light industrial products.

2) The corporate organizational structure:

✓ This is a company with ten years of production in household appliances, with more than 500 engineering talents and 36 subsidiaries all over the world.

✓ ABC has implemented the flat and horizontal organization management structure/linear/tall organization. The top decision level of the company refers to the board of directors and president.

✓ Our company is composed of ten departments.

✓ In addition to customer service, our marketing department is made up of advertising, sales and public relations.

3) Performance:

✓ We have 35% of market share. We will get more next year as our new production line is put into operation.

✓ We have cooperated with two big corporations for more than ten years.

✓ Last year, our net profit from our audited financial statement was 15 million *yuan*.

✓ We have been in business since 1935, and therefore have wide experience in all lines we handle.

3. The definition of「visiting cards」:

Visiting cards may also refer to business cards, which bear the basic information of a company with logo including the major lines and products, contact information such as addresses, telephone numbers, fax numbers, e-mail addresses and websites, as well as the giver's name and position in the company. Usually, the card is somewhat a kind of image representation of oneself. Keep it clean and neat.

4. Tips on making a visiting card:

✓ A Chinese name is quite different from an English name. Usually, the family name (surname, second name) is put at the beginning of a Chinese name followed by the middle name and given name (first name). However, an English name should begin with the given name and end with the family name. Moreover, the initial letter for every part of an English name should be capitalized.

✓ As to the position or job title, the expression should be close to the fixed expression in English. Do not try to translate them at random.

✓ The English expression of place should begin with the smaller place and end up with the largest one.

✓ Different places have different zip codes. Usually, a zip code contains 6 numbers in China. However, that in America should contain two capitalized letters abbreviated for the states, for example: 11203 NY 718 BROOKLYN in which 11203 shows the local zip code of a certain place, NY means New York, 718 is the code for New York, and BROOKLYN is one of the five districts of New York.

5. Sample:

Sovrabh Jain
Company repersetative
+8618857597695

QAFSA GENERAL TRADING(L.L.C)
IMPORTERS, EXPORTERS & WHOLESALERS
Add : In Frount Of Big Shiya Masjid, Bor Dvbai. Po Box:43920
Du Bai (U.A.E)
E-mail : Sourabh bakliwal1991@gmail.com
Sendycool2012@gmail.com

(Dubai) **Manish Inani** +971558982901
(India) **Vishal Inani** +91-9852148223
(China) **Sovrabh Jain** +8618857597695

INANI INTERNATIONAL PVT LTD
Add. Ist Floor, Svzoki Hoose Old R.t.o Road, Gandhi, Nagar
Bhilwara-311001(Rajasthan) India
E-mail: Sourabh bakliwal1991@gmail.com
Sendycool2012@gmail.com

Part Three Reading Task

Reading Task One

Read the following passage and answer the questions.

Incorporated in September of 1991, GF Securities is one of the first full service investment banks and integrated securities brokerage in China. On February 12th, 2010, GF Securities was successfully listed on the Shenzhen Stock Exchange (000776. sz) and by 2013 was the third largest investment bank in China by market capitalization. In 2014, GF Securities was rated a Class A, Grade AA securities company, the highest ranking in the industry. Since 1994, GF Securities has confidently maintained its place as one of the top ten domestic dealers. Currently the company operates 249 business divisions in China, Britain and Canada.

GF Securities has five wholly-owned subsidiaries: GF Futures Co., Ltd., GF Holdings (Hong Kong) Co., Ltd., GF Xinde Investment Management Co., Ltd., GF Qianhe Investment Co., Ltd. and GF Asset Management (Guangdong) Co., Ltd.

As of December 31st, 2014, the company had a registered capital of RMB 5.919 billion, consolidated total assets of RMB 240.01 billion and equity attributable to shareholders of the parent company of RMB 39.61 billion. As reported in its consolidated income statement, the company recorded total operating revenues of RMB 13.395 billion, total profits of RMB 6.649 billion and net profits attributable to shareholders of the parent company of RMB 5.023 billion. The Company has been a leading player in China's securities industry in terms of capital strength and profitability, with a market capitalization surpassing many of its domestic peers'.

Adhering to the principle of prudent operation and standardized management, the company continues to expand through internal growth as well as mergers and acquisitions. With years of remarkable performance measured by key indicators, GF Securities has become one of China's most influential brokerages. Looking ahead, the company will spare no effort in its pursuit of excellence and strive to become a top-notch financial group in China and the Asia-Pacific Region.

Questions:

1. What does GF Securities do?

   _____

2. How many wholly-owned subsidiaries does GF Securities have?

   _____

3. What is the principle of GF Securities?

   _____

4. What is the goal of GF Securities?

   _____

Reading Task Two

Read the following passage and choose the right answers.

   The French claim that visiting cards first appeared in their land in the seventeenth century while the Chinese seek to prove that visiting cards were invented by their ancestors shortly after they had concocted explosive powder. However, the first ever known sample of a visiting card, dating back to 1786, was found in Germany. With the development of certain rules of use, the cards had become common by the nineteenth century.

   Do you know which corner of a visiting card must fold when leaving it with a footman in order to indicate that you have called on to inquire after the master's health? No? Neither do I, but only a hundred years ago this knowledge was as vital for an aristocrat as dancing and polite conversation.

   Visiting cards used to be an indispensable attribute of the etiquette and the rules of their use were as sophisticated as those of cutlery. At that time visiting cards belonged to the notions of such consequence like title, rank, land, horses etc.

First businessmen used their cards as marks of distinction and thus introduced the first modifications in their design. Later, as the growing demand for the cards boosted the development of the printing industry, more and more sophisticated card design patterns appeared.

On the other hand, there appeared an ever-growing social group of private entrepreneurs who had a constant need to exchange their contact information. These pragmatic people started to print out their own cheaper business cards to give them at presentations, exhibitions, conferences, etc.

In the modern business card design, with its developed professional conventions, one can still detect the two conflicting approaches, the fanciful and the functional one. The purpose of the first approach is to show that there is nothing impossible for the card's owner. The more striking by its design and materials and the more sophisticated in its manufacturing technology, the card will be the better. What matters is the card's uniqueness. The content of the card does not matter much either.

The other approach, on the contrary, emphasizes functionality. It is the one that rules in the pragmatic West. And the English name of the item －「business card」－ also focuses on its specific functionality. These cards are essential for those company workers that interact with clients. That is why, on the one hand, you can see a small clerk, a service engineer or even a porter with his own business card and a head of the department without such if he or she does not interact with clients.

Business cards used to be made exclusively of stiff paper (card), but today come in materials from plastics to thin metals and even glass! A name or business card reflects the owner － it should represent visually the company or the person passing it. Take the time to have a closer look at your own cards and decide if they really suit you and your company.

Questions:

1. In which country the first visiting card was found?

A) China. B) France. C) Germany. D) America.

2. What feature of visiting cards does a pragmatic person may focus on?

A) Material. B) Design. C) Uniqueness. D) Functionality.

3. Who are people that are most likely to have visiting cards?

A) Students. B) Sales representatives.

C) Housewives. D) Teachers.

Part Four Supplementary Materials

Useful Expressions: Description of Companies

company image	公司形象	development strategies for the future	未來發展戰略
registered trademark	註冊商標	company market potential	公司市場需要量
registered capital	註冊資金	flexible and varied business operations	靈活多樣的經營方式
enterprise/corporate/company objective	企業發展目標	a stable consumer group	穩定的消費群
well-established company	信譽好的公司	the best price versus performance ratio	最好的性價比
marketing strategies	市場行銷策略	sole proprietorship enterprise/sole investment enterprise	個人獨資企業
state-run enterprise	國營企業	state-owned enterprise	國有企業
collectively-run enterprise	集體企業	township enterprise	鄉鎮企業
private enterprise	私營企業	privately owned individual and commercial enterprise	私營工商業

joint state-private enterprise	公私合營企業	joint venture	合資企業
labor-intensive enterprise	勞動密集型企業	technology-intensive enterprise	技術密集型企業
Sino-foreign joint ventures	中外合資企業	Sino-foreign cooperative enterprise	中外合作企業
foreign-funded enterprise	外方獨資企業		

Useful Sentences: Making a Company Introduction

1. Our company was founded in 2013.

2. Our company specializes in the production of women clothes.

3. ABC Company is a Shenzhen-based consulting firm.

4. We are mainly handling the imports and exports of computers.

5. The total assets of our company are 60 billion *yuan*.

6. The company is a group with first-rate management, first-rate technology, first-rate service, and first-rate staff.

7. Adopting advanced equipment with solid techniques, our high quality products are strictly tested before being put into the market.

8. We sincerely hold the principle of「quality first, customers supreme」in mind when conducting business.

9. There are 80 workers, and more than 100 sets of advanced equipment, taking the leading position in the domestic industry.

10. Our product passed the ISO9001: 2000 international quality system and got CE certificate.

Part Five Assignments

1. Translate the following company introduction into English.

长安汽车源自1862年，是中国近代工业的先驱，隶属于中国南方工业汽车股份有限公司，现有资产1,281亿元、员工8万余人。

长安汽车拥有重庆、北京、上海、江苏、河北、浙江等11大生产基地，30个整车及发动机工厂，年产销汽车260万辆。长期以来，长安汽车稳居中国企业500强。

2. Design a visiting card for yourself. (5 steps)

➢ Step 1: Use 1 minute to imagine what you will be and where you will live five years later.

➢ Step 2: Complete your personal information form in 2–3 minutes, getting some help from Useful Expressions if necessary.

　　　Name: _____

　　　Working unit: _____

　　　Profession and Title: _____

　　　Address: _____

　　　Telephone number: _____

　　　E-mail address: _____

➢ Step 3: Design the card on a piece of paper according to your imagination in 10 minutes.

➢ Step 4: Now exchange your draft with your partner and check his/her draft. Mark them out with the Symbols for Correction.

➢ Step 5: Modify the card according to the partner's mark and then finish the final card.

3. Can you recognize these logos? Give the names of the companies and choose one to make a company introduction.

Unit 6　Memos & Minutes

Objectives

Students are able to:

- understand the definition of a 「memo」 and 「minutes」;
- be familiar with the layout of memos and minutes;
- read and get the major points of memos and minutes;
- accomplish memos and minutes in English.

Part One **Listening Task**

Listen to a conversation between the man and the woman, and then answer the following questions.

1. What information did the woman give the man?

   _____

2. Why didn't the man get the information before?

   _____

3. What is the importance of a memo?

   _____

Part Two General Introduction

1. The definitions of a 「memo」 and 「minutes」:

A *memo* is a short form of the Latin word 「memorandum」. But today it is employed as a kind of communication for inside a company or group, in a word, for inner circulation. Most companies have special memo paper. Unlike letter paper, a memo paper of a company is without the headings (that refers to company's identity, address, telephone, web-site, etc.), but merely with a printed logo.

Minutes, also known as protocols or, informally, notes, are the instant written record of a meeting or hearing. They typically describe the events of the meeting, starting with a list of attendees, a statement of the issues considered by the participants, and related responses or decisions for the issues. Minutes may be created during the meeting by a typist or court reporter, who may use shorthand notation and then prepare the minutes and issue them to the participants afterwards. Alternatively, the meeting can be audio-recorded, video-recorded, or a group's appointed or informally assigned secretary may take notes, with minutes prepared later. Many government agencies use minutes recording software to record and prepare all minutes in real-time.

2. The layout of a memo:

A memo is made of four lines and a body text.

✓ To line (indicating who reads the memo);

✓ From line (indicating who writes the memo);

✓ Subject line (indicating what the topic is for the memo);

✓ Date line (indicating when the memo is written);

✓ The body text is the message.

3. The main factors of minutes:

✓ Name and topic of a meeting;

✓ Date, time and setting of a meeting;

✓ Host of a meeting;

✓ A list of participants;

✓ A list of the persons absent;

✓ Ideas presented for discussion;

✓ Votes or decisions;

✓ Directed action steps;

✓ Note-taker of the minutes.

4. Tips on writing an effective memo:

When you write an effective memo, your words should be informal, clear and brief. As a matter of fact, it's advisable to keep POSE in mind.

P stands for 「positive」, which means a memo should be written in positive tone. For instance, one should write 「Please do be on time」 instead of 「Don't be late for the meeting」. Or replace 「Don't be careless」 with 「You will be appreciated for your carefulness」.

O stands for 「only」, which means a memo should be on only one matter or topic.

S stands for 「short」, which means a memo should be written with short sentences and short paragraphs, or readers will feel tired and even depressed.

E stands for 「easy」, which means easy words are always the first choice in writing a memo. So 「chance」 may be preferable to 「opportunity」.

Notes:

It does not need to be signed, but sometimes having the sender's name at the bottom would be more friendly, or the sender's full name be more formal.

5. Sample study:

Sample I

Memo

To: Mr. Hall

From: Jessica

Date: March 3, 2015

Subject: Feedback of the new system is required.

　　The Training Department is collecting the feedback of the operation of the new system. Please send them the report on:

　　1. How long the system has been working in your Department.

　　2. What jobs it is used for.

　　3. How it is working.

　　The report is expected by 4 p.m. this Friday (7 March).

Sample II

Memo

To: All Department Managers

From: John Green

Date: June 16, 2015

Subject: Discussion on the sales plan of the 3rd quarter, 2015

　　The Sales Department has made a plan for the third quarter of the year. All Department Managers are expected to attend the meeting to discuss the plan. The meeting will be held in the Meeting Room of the Sales Department at 1:00 p.m. on June 19, 2015.

　　If you cannot attend the meeting, please notify the secretary of the Sales Management in advance.

Sample Ⅲ

Minutes of the sales meeting on January 15, 2015 in Conference Room A

Presiding: John Walker, Sales Manager

Present: White Bear, Douglas Carver, Lenny Elizabeth, Jack Porter and Mary Coffin (All are salespersons.)

Absent: Melissa Johnson (salesperson)

Proceedings:

1. Call to order: Meeting called to order at 10:00 a.m. by Chair, John Walker.

2. Discussion:

♦ The sales manager read the sales report in the past three months and pointed out that the sales suffered a great downturn in such a short time.

♦ All the salespersons discussed the reasons why they experienced a great downturn. White Bear and Jack Porter agreed that the main reason should be the unexpected economic crisis. The other salespersons agreed that their products lacked enough propaganda.

♦ The sales manager made a conclusion that the main factor which affected the sales of the products is the lack of enough propaganda. Of course, the economic crisis is one of the external factors.

♦ The sales manager proposed that all of them discuss the measures to change such a situation.

♦ Mary Coffin first proposed that the most important thing should be to take measures to enhance the propaganda of the new product. All the other salespersons agreed.

♦ Finally, the sales manager made a conclusion that only by multiplying their efforts can they succeed in difficulties.

3. Any other business:

The next meeting will be held at the same time and place on February 15, 2015.

The meeting adjourned at 11:30 a.m.

Minutes submitted by Secretary, Joan Lisa.

Part Three Reading Task

Reading Task One

Read the following meeting agenda about sales promotion and answer the questions.

Sales Promotion Meeting Agenda

    Date/Time: January 15, 2015, 10:00 a.m. – 11:30 a.m.

    Location: Conference Room A

    Attendees:

- ◆ John Walker – Sales Manager
- ◆ All the salespersons

Objectives:

♦ Review the sales in the past three months.

♦ Find out the reasons why our sales suffer a downturn.

♦ How to change such a terrible situation.

Schedule:

10:00 to 10:15	Review speech – sales manager
10:15 to 10:45	Discussion of the reasons – all the salespersons
10:45 to 11:00	Conclusion of the reasons – sales manager
11:00 to 11:15	Discussion of the ways – all the salespersons
11:15 to 11:30	Conclusion of the ways – sales manager

Roles/ Responsibilities:

Note-taking: Joan Venn

Questions:

1. What elements are included in a meeting agenda?

   _____

2. When and where will they have a meeting?

   _____

3. Who will attend the meeting?

   _____

4. What are objectives of the meeting?

   _____

5. Who will make the review speech at the meeting?

   _____

Reading Task Two

Read the following passage and decide whether the following statements are true or false. Write (T) for true and (F) for false.

How to Prepare for a Meeting

Preparing is very important in having a successful meeting. Meetings are also a major part of most careers, so it can be a big deal! Follow these steps to help encourage success in your next meeting.

1. Knowing how to prepare for a meeting is important for all employees and critical for any manager or leader. Knowing when not to have a meeting is equally important.

2. Decide the type of meeting you are going to have: informational; creative; decision; motivational.

3. Determine the roles and ask those participants to accept them. The roles are the following: leader; facilitator; recorder; timer; participants.

4. Prepare a notice. This should include the date, time, agenda, and venue of the meeting. Distribute the notice to the members in good time for the meeting.

5. Attach the minutes of the previous meeting (if there has been one). This gives members the chance to bring up anything they do not understand or disagree with.

6. Get basic items in place. Set out chairs and tables before the meeting begins. Provide pens and paper for everyone. Place a pitcher of water in the middle of the table and put glasses around the table.

7. Call the meeting to order. This means the chairperson asks everyone to stop talking as the meeting is about to begin. Determine the quarterly goals for the team. The agenda is a list of the topics you'll address to get to that objective, with a time limit to keep you on track. For example: 1) Review the status of last quarter's goals (15 minutes); 2) Round-table suggestions for goals (20 minutes); 3) Pick top 5 goals (10 minutes).

8. Pass around the attendance book or sheet of paper and ask everyone attending to sign

their names at the beginning of the meeting.

9. Ask the minutes secretary to write down the main points of the meeting for typing up later.

10. Ask if anyone has any other business, known as AOB, at the end of the formal meeting. Set a date for the next meeting and formally close the meeting.

Questions:

( ) 1. It is equally important to know when to have a meeting and when not to.

( ) 2. It is not necessary to prepare pens or paper for everyone.

( ) 3. Attaching the minutes of the previous meeting gives members the chance to bring up anything they do not understand or disagree with.

( ) 4. The attendance book or sheet of paper should be signed at the end of the meeting.

( ) 5. AOB in the meeting minutes stands for Any Other Business.

Part Four　Supplementary Materials

Useful Expressions: Meetings

on the occasion of	借此……之際	declare ... open/declare the commencement of ...	宣布……揭幕
deliver/make an opening/closing speech	致揭幕/閉幕詞	declare ... the conclusion/closing of	宣布……閉幕
in conclusion/ finally/ at last	最后	meeting agenda	會議議程
meeting minutes	會議紀要	convention center	會議中心
the inaugural session	開幕式	sales convention	銷售會議

academic exchange forum	學術交流論壇	a fruitful meeting	很有成效的會議
the people's congress	人民代表大會	the Democratic National Convention	民主黨全國代表大會
the youth congress	青年代表大會		

Useful Sentences: Writing a Memo

1. Please note that individual statistics are not disclosed and this is for internal only.

2. Further suggestions will be appreciated so that the program can be more fruitful.

3. I'd like you to attend the meeting at 10:00 a. m. Saturday.

4. Would you please advise if you agree with this approach?

5. May I remind you that we are in want of a telephone for each dormitory?

6. This is the reminder of your being accepted to join the workshop scheduled for 22-24 December, 2015.

7. You are kindly requested to submit the letter of intent on the date no later than 1st August.

8. Hope this is okay with you. If not, let me know by e-mail ASAP.

9. We seek your assistance to cascade / reply this message to your staff.

10. If anybody would like to take holidays together with the Spring Festival holidays, please inform your manager in advance.

Part Five Assignment

You are required to write a memo according to the information given in Chinese below. Your memo should be in 100 to 120 words.

該備忘錄是 G&P 國家貿易公司計劃部 Edward 先生於 2007 年 3 月 10 日寫給人事部 Owen 先生的。備忘錄包括以下內容：

- 公司急於在中國擴大市場，現計劃招聘一名銷售經理。
- 應聘者要求：具有市場策劃方面的實際經驗；2 年以上工作經驗；良好的英語以及普通話聽、說、寫能力；精通計算機軟件操作；有良好的人際關係、懂撰寫報告及演講的技巧。

Words for reference：**planning department**；**HR department**；**sales manager**；**marketing planning**；**Mandarin**（普通話）；**proficient**（精通）

Unit Seven　Business Correspondence

Objectives

Students are able to:

- understand what a business letter is;
- get to know the elements and styles of business letters;
- be familiar with different types of business letters;
- acquire some useful expressions in writing business letters;
- write effective business letters.

Part One　Listening Task

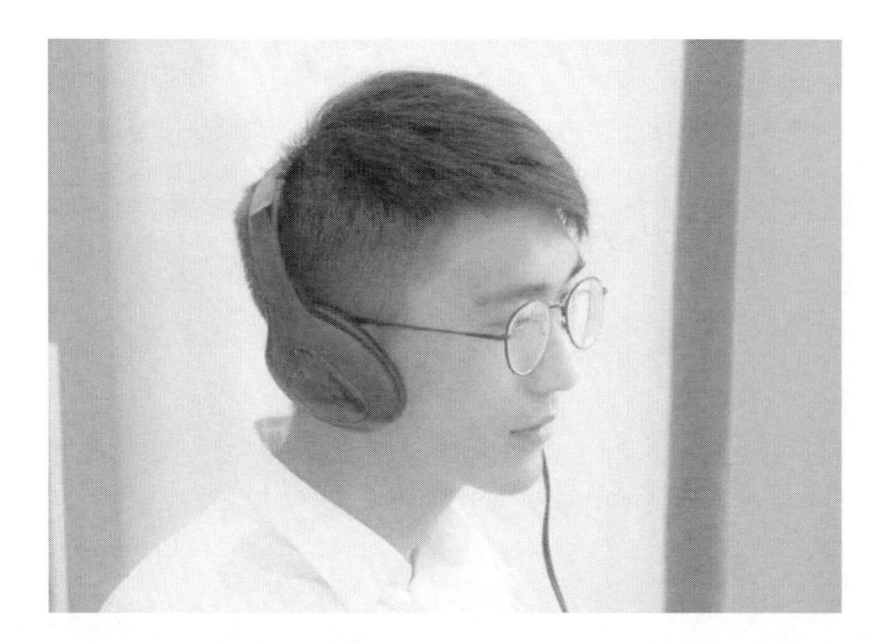

Listen to the conversation and complete the following summary with suitable words and expressions.

The woman is writing a letter to one of her (1) _____, but she wonders how to get it started, because she does not know the name of the (2) _____ person. The man suggests that if it is not (3) _____, the letter could be written like this:

To whom it may (4) _____,

We are very (5) _____ for your continued (6) _____. Regarding our new (7) _____ line, we would like to announce a special price (8) _____. Please find enclosed our (9) _____ service survey. Please return the survey without (10) _____ /at your earliest (11) _____.

Yours (12) _____,

Mary White

Part Two General Introduction

1. The definition of a business letter:

A business letter is usually a letter from one company to another, or between such organizations and their customers, clients and other external parties. The overall style of letters depends on the relationship between the parties concerned. Business letters can have many types of contents, for example, to request direct information or action from another party, to order supplies from a supplier, to point out a mistake by the letter's recipient, to reply directly to a request, to apologize for a wrong, or to convey goodwill.

The business-letter format is very important for communicating formally with a company. You shouldn't write in the same voice as when you write to your family or friends. A business letter needs to be more formal.

2. Elements of a business letter:

Standard parts: letterhead (can be substituted with a return address in an individual-to-business letter), date, inside address or the recipient's address, salutation, the body of the letter, complimentary close, signature block.

Optional parts: the attention line (具體收信人), the subject line (事由), the reference notation (案號), the enclosure (附件), the carbon copy notation (抄送), the postscript (附言).

3. Styles of business letters:

Full block style（齊頭式）: The full block format is the simplest format; All of the writing is flush against the left margin.

```
Dixie Cleverelle
SavbizCor Ltd
28 Green St., Suite 14
Upstate, NY 10947

October 27, 2006

Ms. Margaret Edwards
Barnelli Ltd
48 Stanstead Road
London SE27 1HF

For the Attention of Financial Manager

Dear Ms. Edwards:

I wanted to take this opportunity to thank you for the excellent job you did in arranging
financing for our project. We appreciate the fact that you made yourself available for
discussion seven days a week. We were impressed by your thourough knowledge of
financing and investment banking.

We have been dealing with our new financial institution for about a week now. The
advantages of association with this institution are already apparent. I feel as though
we have taken a quantum leap forward in progress.

I would not hesitate to retain your services again and to recommend your firm to any
company seeking the best representation.

Sincerely yours,

D. Cleverelle

Dixie Cleverelle,
President
```

Indented or Semi-Block Style (縮進式)：In the US the indented letter does look a little outdated. However, a lot of companies still use it.

Imperial Stationery Ltd
258 North Hampton Road Manhasset, NY 10847   (914) 375-2788

January 4, 2007

Ms. Ashley Nickols
Savbizcor Ltd
28 Green St., Suite 11
Upstate, NY 10947

Dear Ms. Nickols:

  Thank you for ordering 15 cases of premium paper from Imperial Stationery Ltd. Your order has been shipped and should reach you within the next five business days.

  Find enclosed your total bill for the above order amounting to $794.85, and the check for $23.85 is your refund. Because you paid in advance, we are giving you 3 percent cash discount and we also are paying for shipping and handling.

  Imperial Stationery is pleased to add you to its list of customers. We look forward to your next order.

         Sincerely,

         J. O'Conelly

         Jennifer O'Conelly
         Customer Service

2 Enclosures

Modified block style（修正式）: Modified block business letters use a slightly different format from the full block business letters. In the modified block style the return address, date, complimentary closing and the signature line are slightly to the right of the center of the paper. The return address has become uncommon for business letters, and it is usually substituted by a letterhead.

```
                                        Gregory Donaldson
                                        Minoan Inc
                                        247 Madison Ave., Suite 2103
                                        New York, NY 10015

                                        December 3, 2006


Dixie Cleverelle
Savbizcor Ltd
28 Green St., Suite 14
Upstate, NY 10947

Dear Ms. Cleverelle:

The first shipment of equipment from Savbizcor Ltd has arrived. We are delighted
with every piece. Therefore, we decided to make our initial purchase larger than
anticipated. I am attaching our purchase order No. 8930 for additional goods totaling
list price $700,000.

Since you already have a copy of our Procurement Guidelines, I shall not attach them
to this order. As before, we will establish a letter of credit. Please inform me of
shipping dates.

                                        Sincerely,

                                        G. Donaldson

                                        Gregory Donaldson,
                                        Chief Procurement Officer


Enclosure: Purchase Order No. 8930
```

4. Common types of business letters:

- ✓ Acknowledgement Letter
- ✓ Apology Letter
- ✓ Appreciation Letter
- ✓ Complaint Letter
- ✓ Inquiry Letter
- ✓ Order Letter
- ✓ Letter of Recommendation

Notes:

These are the common types of business letters. The number may even increase since there are several reasons a company or an individual would need to write it.

5. Sample study:

Sample I: A complaint letter

Dear Customer Service Representative,

I am writing to complain about the bad delivery service of your company.

The IBM Desktop computer we ordered from your store two weeks ago finally arrived yesterday. There were not any signs of damage to the packing case at all, but when we opened it, we found, much to our surprise, that the back cover had been cracked and the screen had been scratched.

In view of this, I have decided to make a formal complaint against your delivery service. I sincerely hope that you will replace this computer as soon as possible. If this is not possible, I will have no alternative but to insist on a full refund.

I would appreciate anything you can do to help us in this matter.

Sincerely yours,

Lucy Chen

Sample II: An inquiry letter

Dear Sir or Madam,

We are an import/export company with three years' experience, specializing in European trade. The Bank of China has suggested we contact you in order to explore whether we could help with your import/export needs.

We invite you to send us details of goods that you would like to be able to sell in China. We will be glad to send you an interim report of marketing possibilities in our market.

Also, if you would like to send us a list of those articles you are interested in obtaining from China, we will look into supply possibilities on your behalf. We can guarantee a preliminary report within two weeks and if suitable supplies exist, we would expect to be able to send you samples within four weeks of your initial order.

If there is any other information that you require or if we can help in any other way, please do not hesitate to contact us.

Yours faithfully,
Wang Hua
Sales Manager

Sample III: An appreciation letter

Liu Ming

Foreign Trade Minister

Beijing, China

Dear Minister,

I am writing this letter to thank you for your warm hospitality accorded to me and my delegation during our recent visit to your beautiful country. I would also like to thank you for your interesting discussion with me which I have found very informative and useful.

During the entire visit, my delegation and I were overwhelmed by the enthusiasm expressed by your business representatives on cooperation with U. S. A. I sincerely hope we could have more exchanges like this one when we would be able to continue our interesting discussion on possible ways to expand our bilateral economic and trade relations and bring our business people together.

　　I am looking forward to your early visit to U. S. A. when I will be able to pay back some of the hospitality I received during my memorable stay in your beautiful country. With kind personal regards.

Faithfully yours,
David White
Minister of Economic Cooperation

Part Three　Reading Task

Reading Task One

Read through the following passage and answer the questions.

A good business letter is polite, straightforward and brief. If possible, it should be limited to one single-spaced typewritten page. Because it is so brief, a business letter is often judged on small, but important things: format, grammar, punctuation, openings and closings. A business letter is not the place to try out fancy fonts or experimental writing styles.

In some cases, a business letter has the same function as the promotional newsletters which are used to motivate consumers to react to an offer made via direct letters or emails. The skill of writing letters is not always an easy one to acquire, yet letter writing remains an important activity in our business. The first impression left by our letter is not only critical to the success of our message, but also to the image we wish to present.

A well-written business letter builds trust and confidence on a company and a brand. Each sentence within the letter should be well selected because a business letter can increase your image with prospective and presented clients. By providing valuable information, the readers will recognize you as an expert in your field or product. This is probably the hardest part and also the reason why many companies hire professional writers.

Questions:

1. What are the features of a good business letter?

2. How is a business letter judged?

3. Why is the first impression of a business letter so important?

4. Why do many companies hire professional writers?

_____

Reading Task Two

Read the following letters and decide whether the following statements are true or false. Write (T) for true and (F) for false.

A Specific Enquiry for Silk Blouses

Dear Sirs,

    Many reports have been received from our sales agents in Hong Kong, that there are very brisk demand for the captioned garments.

    We are pleased to learn that your mill is the most well-known producer of this item in China. We, therefore, are writing to you for quotations for Silk Blouses of all three sizes: large, medium, and small. As expected, the quantity of our orders to be placed will be very large. So we hope you can quote us your best prices.

    When quoting, please state your prices on both FOBC 2% and CIFC 2% Los Angeles. Please be assured that your prices should be competitive, and we will place our orders with you and open L/C in your favor in time.

    Your prompt reply to this enquiry will be appreciated.

Yours truly,
Jack Lee
ABC Company

Reply to the Enquiry Above

Dear Sirs,

  We are pleased to learn from your enquiry dated November 5th that you are interested in our silk blouses.

  We are now in a position to supply you with our wide range of Silk Blouses we make for all age groups. Enclosed please find our Quotations Sheet No. 257 covering different sizes and colors that can be shipped from stock. All the prices quoted are net, to which please add your commission. If you ask for orders over US $ 50,000, we will offer you the quantity discount of 4%.

  We usually accept confirmed, irrevocable L/C payable by draft at sight. We are confident that you will find a ready sale for our products in your market. Any order you may place with us will have our prompt attention.

Yours truly,

Jim Liu

PNG Silk Company

Questions:

( ) 1. Silk blouses in all sizes are needed by ABC Company.

( ) 2. The style of both the letters is modified block style.

( ) 3. Silk blouses for all age groups are produced by PNG Silk Company.

( ) 4. The prices quoted on Quotations Sheet No. 257 include the cost prices and commission for ABC Company.

( ) 5. If ABC Company places an order of US $ 80,000, a quantity discount of 4% will be offered.

Part Four Supplementary Materials

Useful Expressions

1. Expressing the purpose for a letter

   1) I am writing to confirm your order placed via email on April 1st.

   2) This is regarding our quotation dated November 2nd and our mail offer dated November 8th concerning the supply of widgets.

   3) I am writing to apologize for not attending the appointment which I promised.

   4) I am writing to complain about the service offered by your company.

2. Providing requirements

   1) I would be grateful if you could send me the copy of the contract as soon as possible.

   2) I would appreciate it if you could give our counteroffer your most favorable consideration.

3. Apologizing

   1) I regret to inform you that your contract will not be renewed.

   2) I am afraid that we are unable to offer you the job.

   3) I apologize for the delaying of your ordered goods.

   4) We are sorry we cannot send you immediately the catalogue and price list for which you asked in your letter of March 10th.

   5) I was very concerned when I received your letter of yesterday complaining that the central heating system in your new house had not been completed by the date promised.

4. Inquiries and replies

   1) We are interested in obtaining catalogues and price lists of your embroidered linen products.

2) We welcome your enquiry of August 16th and thank you for your interest in our embroidered linen products.

5. Reminding the recipient of the attachment

    1) Enclosed is our new price list which will come into effect at the end of this month.

    2) We have much pleasure in enclosing a quotation sheet for our products and trust that their high quality will induce you to place a trial order.

Part Five　Assignment

Translate the following apology letter into Chinese.

Dear Sir,

    Thank you for your letter of 20 May referring to your order No. 252. We are glad to hear that the consignment was delivered promptly.

    We regret, however, that case No. 46 did not contain the goods you ordered. We have investigated the matter and find that we did make a mistake in putting the order together. We have arranged for the correct goods to be dispatched to you at once. The relevant documents will be mailed to you as soon as they are ready. Please keep case No. 46 and its contents until called for by our agents who have been informed of the situation.

    We apologize for the inconvenience caused by our error.

Yours faithfully,
Tony Smith
Chief Seller

Unit Eight   Travel for Business

Objectives

Students are able to:

- know the definition and purpose of a business travel;
- know how to prepare for a business travel and apply for a business visa;
- understand daily conversations about business travel;
- acquire some useful expressions during the process of business travel.

Part One Listening Task

Listening Task One

Listen to a dialogue between the two speakers and finish the following exercises. Tick ($\checkmark$) the points that are mentioned in their conversion and cross ($\times$) the points that are not mentioned.

(　) 1. I will set out to Paris with my assistant.

(　) 2. I booked a round-trip ticket.

(　) 3. I will return on July 21.

Listening Task Two

Listen to a dialogue between the two speakers and answer the following questions.

1. What should the woman prepare for her American trip?

   _____

2. What is she going to do in America?

   _____

3. What did the man ask the woman to do?

   _____

Part Two   General Introduction

1. What is a business travel?

A business travel or business trip is a travel done in the course of business or work, other than the daily commuting between home and workplace.

2. The purpose of a business travel:

✓ to visit customers or suppliers;

✓ to attend meetings at other company locations;

✓ to expand business and find opportunities.

3. How to apply for a business visa:

The necessary procedures of applying for a visa:

✓ a valid passport;

✓ an application in a relative embassy with a passport photo;

✓ an invitation from the company in the other country;

✓ a certificate authorizing the business trip from the superior authorities indicating the dates in accordance with the passport;

✓ a certificate from your company indicating the back time;

✓ a list of people together with you indicating the details of them;

✓ one copy of the company's license;

✓ a personal financing certificate;

✓ a contract or orders certificate between the foreign country and your company.

4. Visa sample:

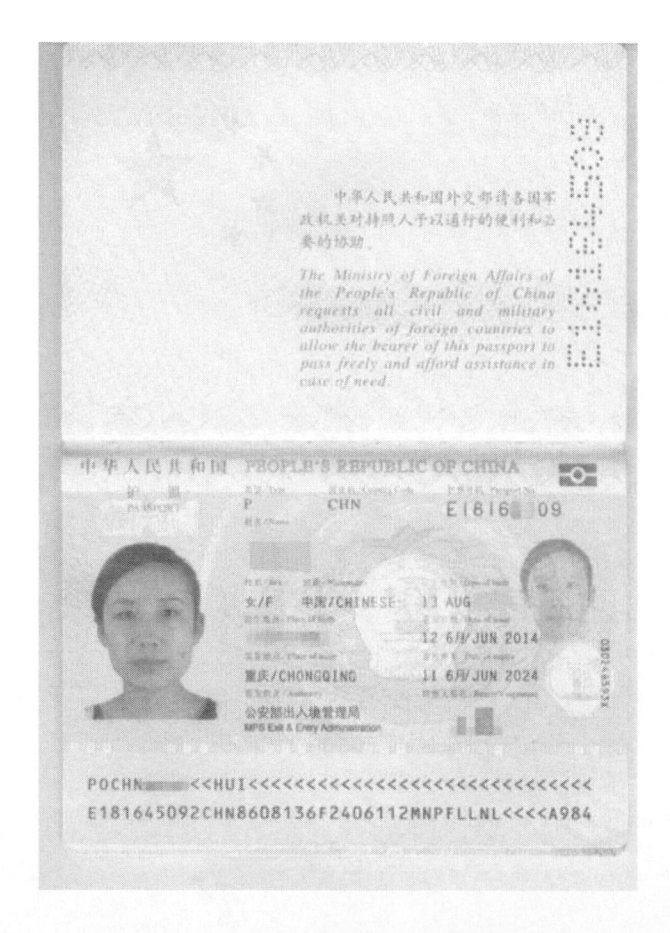

Part Three Reading Task

Reading Task One

Read the following conversation about applying for a business visa and answer the questions.

Coleman: What special skills do you have?

Ray: I have had four American English teachers. I took part in cultural exchanges with many of them. Here are their references about my English and business skills.

Coleman: I see. Such references will help you to get the visa. To double-check, I must ask if you have any criminal record. Have you ever been convicted of a crime in China?

Ray: I am glad to say I have never broken the law. In addition, I have been studying the laws of the United States so that there will be no problem when I go there. I have been and always will be an honest, law-abiding man.

Coleman: Are you aware many Chinese travel to USA on temporary visas, then immigrate after that? Do you promise not to do that?

Ray: I can assure you I would never leave my family. As you can see from my application I have verification from my host company that they will be responsible for seeing that I return to China within two years.

Coleman: Please sign this form saying you have not lied during the interview today or on your application. The truth is important to us.

Ray: Ditto, the truth is important to me too. It would be my pleasure to sign the form.

Coleman: Do you have any questions for us?

Ray: Of course, thank you. Can you tell me anything else I can do to prepare myself to go abroad?

Coleman: Your best bet is to start reading an American newspaper. Try to get a newspaper that is published near your destination. Baltimore, Maryland has a famous paper called *The Baltimore Sun*. Start reading.

Ray: Also, sir, how long will it take you to make your decision on my visa?

Coleman: It will take about two to three weeks. We will call you with an answer.

Ray: Thank you very much, sir. You have been more than helpful.

Coleman: You're welcome, Mr. Lee. But I am not promising anything.

Questions:

1. How is Ray demonstrating his special skills?

   _____

2. Is Ray an honest, law-abiding man?

   _____

3. How long will Ray stay in America at the most?

_____

4. What suggestion has been given by Coleman to Ray for him to do some preparations to go abroad?

_____

5. How long will it take to decide on Ray's visa?

_____

Reading Task Two

Read the following passage and decide whether the following statements are true or false. Write (T) for true and (F) for false.

Cultural practices, cultural differences, local manners, and mores: Traveling the globe can be a behavioral minefield, even when you have the best intentions. Everything from greeting to eating can be an opportunity to do the wrong thing, and not only embarrass yourself, but offend your host countrymen. Look out for the following cultural mistakes and try to avoid them while going abroad.

1. Touching Someone

Where it's offensive: Korea, Thailand, China, Europe, and the Middle East.

What's offensive: Personal space varies as you travel the globe. In Mediterranean countries, if you refrain from touching someone's arm when talking to them or if you don't greet them with kisses or a warm embrace, you'll be considered cold. But backslap someone who isn't a family member or a good friend in Korea, and you'll make them uncomfortable. In Thailand, the head is considered sacred—never even pat a child on the head.

2. Blowing Your Nose

Where it's offensive: Japan, China, Saudi Arabia, and France.

What's offensive: Some cultures find it disgusting to blow your nose in public—especially at the table. The Japanese and Chinese are also repelled by the idea of a handkerchief.

3. Talking over Dinner

Where it's offensive: Africa, Japan, Thailand, China, and Finland.

What's offensive: In some countries, like China, Japan, and some African nations, the food's the thing, so don't start chatting about your day's adventures while everyone else is digging into dinner. You'll likely be met with silence—not because your group is unfriendly, but because mealtimes are for eating, not talking. Also avoid conversations in places a country might consider sacred or reflective—churches in Europe, temples in Thailand, and saunas in Finland.

4. Removing Your Shoes ... or Not

Where it's offensive: Hawaii, the South Pacific, Korea, China, and Thailand.

What's offensive: Take off your shoes when arriving at the door of a London dinner party and the hostess will find you uncivilized, but fail to remove your shoes before entering a home in Asia, Hawaii, or the Pacific Islands and you'll be considered disrespectful. Not only does shoe removal very practically keep sand and dirt out of the house, it's a sign of leaving the outside world behind.

5. Knowing Your Right from Your Left

Where it's offensive: India, Morocco, Africa, the Middle East.

What's offensive: Many cultures still prefer to eat using traditional methods—their hands. In these cases, food is often offered communally, which is why it's important to wash your hands before eating and observe the right-hand-is-for-eating and the left-hand-is-for-other-duties rule. If you eat with your left hand, expect your fellow diners to be mortified. And when partaking from a communal bowl, stick to a portion that's closest to you. Do not get greedy and plunge your hand into the center.

Once you are on the ground of a different country, remain highly sensitive to native behavior. Never be completely surprised by anything; try to take it in stride, and don't feel offended if something seems offensive—like queue jumping. After all, this is a global village, and we are all very different.

Questions:

(　) 1. In China, if you don't greet others with kisses or a warm embrace, you'll be considered cold.

(　) 2. Touching someone on the head who isn't a family member or a good friend in Korea, you'll make them uncomfortable.

(　) 3. In France it is disgusting to blow your nose in public.

(　) 4. Chatting in saunas in Finland is impolite.

(　) 5. Take off your shoes when arriving at the door of a London dinner party and the hostess will find you civilized.

(　) 6. In Morocco, if you eat with your left hand, your fellow diners will feel mortified.

Part Four　Supplementary Materials

Useful Expressions: Airports

Beijing Capital International Airport (PEK)	北京首都國際機場
Shanghai Pudong International Airport (PVG)	上海浦東機場
Shanghai Hongqiao Airport (SHA)	上海虹橋機場
London Heathrow Airport (LHR)	倫敦希思羅機場
Manchester Airport (MAN)	曼徹斯特機場
Charles de Gaulle Airport (CDG)	巴黎戴高樂機場

Frankfurt International Airport（FRA）	法蘭克福國際機場
Aeropuerto de Madrid-Barajas（MAD）	馬德里巴拉哈斯機場
Copenhagen Airport（CPH）	哥本哈根機場
Zürich Unique Airport（ZRH）	蘇黎世國際機場
Narita International Airport（NRT）	東京成田國際機場
Kansai International Airport（KIX）	大阪關西國際機場
Incheon International Airport（ICN）	仁川國際機場
Busan Gimhae International Airport（PUS）	釜山金海國際機場
Don Mueang International Airport（DMK）	廊曼國際機場

Useful Sentences: Travel for Business

1. I want to book an airplane ticket to Paris.

2. I want a package deal including airfare and hotel.

3. You want to go first class or economy class?

4. Which gate should we board the plane?

5. When should I check in?

6. I'd like to apply for a visa to America.

7. What's the weight limit?

8. I'm going to have to confiscate these.

9. We have to handle fresh fruit with kid gloves.

10. Here is your declaration form.

Part Five Assignments

1. Please talk about one of your most impressive travels by answering the following questions:
   - Where have you been?
   - How did you get there?
   - Who did you go along with?
   - How did you spend it?
   - What makes you think it impressive?
2. Try to find out the similarities and differences in applying for a business visa in China and in America.

Unit Nine   Making Reservations

Objectives

Students are able to:

- know how to make reservations;

- grasp the key language points in making reservations and learn how to use them in context;

- make reservations freely during life and business travel.

Part One **Listening Task**

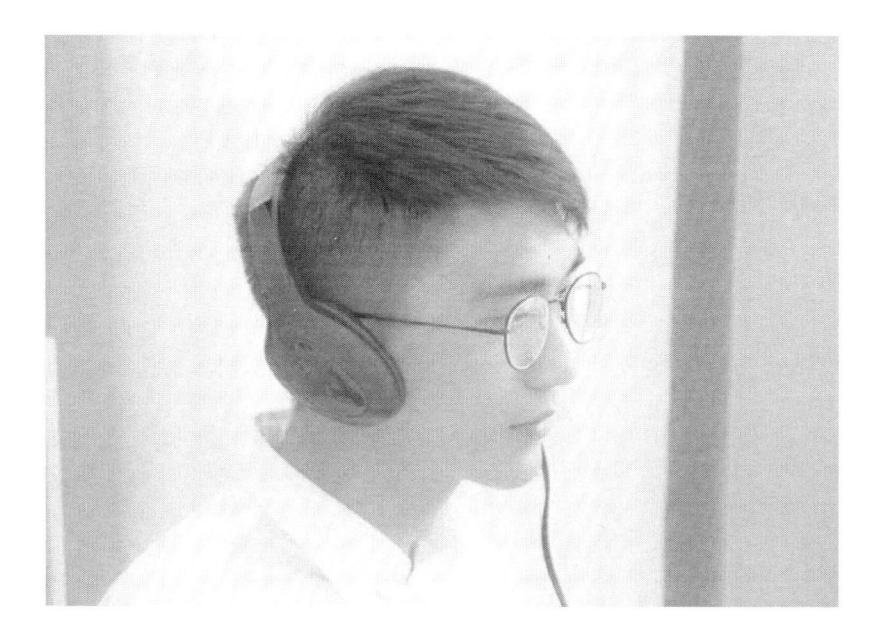

Listen to the dialogue between the two speakers and finish the following exercises.

1. What is the possible relationship between the two speakers?

2. What are they talking about?

3. List the most important information mentioned in the conversation.

4. Please describe the procedure of room reservation.

Part Two Speaking Task

Brainstorm:

Questions for Discussion

1. How can we reserve a room in modern life?

2. Match Chinese with English.

Resident Hotel	商業型酒店
Convention Hotel	常住型酒店
Casino Hotel	會議型酒店
Bed & Breakfast Hotel	度假型酒店
Motel	賭場型酒店
Commercial Hotel	汽車旅館
Resort Hotel	家庭式飯店

3. Identify the room types.

(　　　)　　　　　　　　　　　　(　　　)

(   )

Part Three Reading Task

Reading Task One

Read the dialogue and choose the right answers.

    Clerk: Good afternoon. Reservations. May I help you?

Xinrong: Hello, this is Xinrong calling from Asian Drinks Company. I'd like to know if you have rooms available for the nights from December 11 to December 16. We are going to have a business fair.

Clerk: May I ask how many people there will be in the party, sir?

Xinrong: Ten persons.

Clerk: What kind of rooms would you like to reserve, sir?

Xinrong: One suite and nine single.

Clerk: Will you need the room with bath or without?

Xinrong: Is there any difference in price?

Clerk: A single room with bath is $80 per night, without bath $55; and a suite with bath is $150 per night, without bath $120.

Xinrong: Without bath then. You have some sort of washing facilities, I think?

Clerk: Yes, of course. So that's one suite, nine single without bath, arriving on the 11th of December and checking out on the 16th. Asian Drinks Company.

Xinrong: That's right. Well, is there a special rate for a group reservation?

Clerk: Yes, we can offer you a 20% discount. By the way, could you tell me how you will be settling the account, please?

Xinrong: The Company will cover all the expenses and we'll send you a check soon.

Clerk: Thank you for calling, sir. We look forward to welcoming you.

Questions:

1. What kind of rooms will the company reserve?

A) One suite without shower and nine single with bath.

B) One suite and nine single without bath.

C) One suite with bath and nine single without bath.

D) One suite and nine single with showers.

2. If the company will stay at the hotel from December 11 to December 16 for five nights,

how much will the company have to pay for?

A) $ 4,200.   B) $ 3,075.   C) $ 2,580.   D) $ 2,460.

3. How will the company make the payment?

A) Credit card.   B) Cash.   C) Check.   D) Transfer.

Reading Task Two

Read the passage and answer the following questions.

How to Make a Hotel Reservation

If you aren't someone who takes vacations that require a hotel stay, or travels for business or your kids' sporting events, you may not know how to make a hotel reservation. By following these simple steps, you can ensure that your hotel meets your needs and expectations when you arrive.

First, check rates and make a hotel reservation as far in advance of the departure date as possible. Hotels tend to raise rates as availability declines; however, it is possible to get a last minute deal.

Second, use an online travel site to identify hotels in the city you are visiting or near a specific attraction, address or airport. Sites that book hotels, flights, rental cars, vacation packages and more include Orbitz. Com, Expedia. Com and Travelocity. Com. These sites have features that make it easy to adjust dates and see how it affects hotel rates. Hotels. Com (an Expedia company) and HotelDiscounts. Com specialize in lodgings but also book vacation packages. Sidestep. Com is a search engine for other travel sites and makes it easy to compare hotel reservations and other rates. If you aren't picky about arrival and departure dates or location, you might consider Priceline. Com. However, you won't know which hotel you are staying in until you book it.

Third, determine whether you need a standard room, one-bedroom, two-bedroom or something larger.

Four, identify what amenities you need. In-room conveniences to consider include high-speed Internet, a refrigerator, a kitchen or kitchenette, and a pull-out sleeper sofa. Some hotels will bring a crib or cot into the room if you need it. Hotel amenities might include an indoor or outdoor pool, fitness center, business center, restaurants and room service.

Five, enter your arrival and departure dates as well as how many adults and children will be staying in the room.

Six, narrow down the list to one or two hotels with the amenities you need and the best rates, and then go to those hotel websites to check rates there. Compare rates with discounts (e.g., for seniors, AAA members, frequent flyer members) and taxes applied. If you are bringing pets, verify that pets are allowed and whether an additional fee is charged. Take into account whether a free breakfast is included, or a happy hour offers free drinks and/or food.

Seven, look at the photos and virtual tours available online to get a feel for what the hotel and its rooms look like. You may need to call the hotel to get specific information, such as the year built/remodeled, check-in/check-out times and cancellation policy.

Eight, book the hotel room online or by phone. You will need to give a credit card number, but the card will not be charged unless you don't cancel according to the cancellation policy.

Nine, print or write down your confirmation number and bring it with you on the trip.

Tips:

1. When calling the hotel directly to make a hotel reservation, don't be afraid to ask for a better deal or free room upgrade.

2. Contact the hotel's sales department if you need to book a hotel reservation for a group.

Warnings:

1. Before you book a hotel reservation online, check whether there is a booking fee. It may be cheaper to use the hotel website, rather than a travel site.

2. Most hotels will charge you at least one night stay if you do not cancel a reservation within the time allotted. Some hotels allow you to cancel the same day as check-in, but others

require a day or more notice.

Questions:

1. List the people who are most likely to make hotel reservations.

   _____

2. List as many websites available to book hotels as possible.

   _____

3. What amenities should one take into account for conveniences when making hotel reservations?

   _____

4. Will your credit card be charged if you cancel the reservation according to the cancellation policy?

   _____

5. What is the possible way to get a cheaper reservation?

   _____

Part Four Supplementary Materials

Useful Expressions: Room Types & Service

single room	單人間	mountain-view room	山景房
twin room/double room	雙人間	bell service	應接服務

standard room	標準間	room service	客房服務
suite	套間	food service	用餐服務
room with kitchen	帶廚房客房	laundry service	洗衣服務
handicapped room	殘疾人客房	operator service	電話總機服務
adjoining room	相鄰房	Do not disturb.	請勿打擾
ocean-view room	海景房	lake-view room	江景房

Useful Sentences: Making Reservations

1. I'd like to reserve a double room for two nights.

2. I'd like to know if you have vacant rooms for us.

3. Are you single or with a company?

4. How many people are there in your party altogether?

5. Would you like to have a single room or double room?

6. What kind of room would you like, with a bath or without?

7. I'd like to book a room with a shower. Do you have a vacant one?

8. The suites are too expensive. A single room is okay.

9. Could you tell me the price of your single rooms?

10. I'm sorry, but the hotel is full on that date.

Part Five Assignment

Complete the following form according to the given information.

來自上海絲綢進出口貿易公司的 John Brown, David Smith, Helen Woods and Mary White 將於 2015 年 11 月 4~6 日到重慶參加絲綢展覽會。秘書 Vivian 為他們在重慶市揚

子島酒店預訂了帶淋浴的兩間標間，並為 11 月 5 日預訂了一間會議室。他們將用公司的信用卡付款。電話是 021-88996263，傳真是 021-88996262，電子郵箱是 vivian@163.com。

Reservation Form

Hotel Name: Yangtze Island Hotel (Chongqing)

Address: Jiefangbei Pedestrian Street

Tel: 023-60638888

Guest's Name	
Time to check in	
Time to check out	
Room type and number	
Payment	
Tel	
Fax	
E-mail	

Unit Ten   Having Business Dinners

Objectives

Students are able to:

- understand the basic information of business entertainment;
- know the basic business table manners;
- effectively use communication skills to:

1. invite business associates to have dinner;

2. order Western/Chinese food;

3. comment on food;

4. propose a toast during dinner.

Part One Listening Task

Listen to the dialogue between the two speakers and fill in the blanks.

Dialogue:

A: Good morning, Mr. Brown.

B: Good morning. Nice to meet you.

A: Me too. I'm (1) _____ whether you are free on Wednesday night.

B: Let me check my schedule. I don't have an (2) _____ then.

A: Great. I'd like to invite you to have a dinner.

B: It's very kind of you. I have not had Chinese food before.

A: What about Roast Duck? We are planning to hold a banquet in your honor at Quanjude Restaurant.

B: I am (3) _____ to go. I have heard it is famous for its Roast Duck.

A: Exactly. What time would be (4) _____ for you?

B: How about 6 p.m.?

A: OK. I will wait for you at the lounge of the hotel at that time.

B: Fine. Thank you for your invitation.

Having dinner

A: I am (5) _____ you have come. Take a seat.

B: Thank you for your (6) _____.

A: What would you like to drink? This is world-famous Maotai. Do you want to have a try?

B: No. Thanks. (7) _____ is too strong for me. Just a glass of red wine.

A: We have just (8) _____. Shall we raise a toast to a good cooperation?

B: Cheers. I hope we will have more orders to come.

A: Sure. I would like to propose a toast to (9) _____.

B: To our health and friendship.

A: (10) _____.

B: Please make yourself at home.

Part Two Speaking Task

Speaking Task One

Brainstorm: Entertainment

1. Why do we entertain our clients/associates?

2. What kinds of activities do we usually have to entertain our business partners?

Speaking Task Two

Discussion: Business Dinner

1. Which meal do you select to entertain your clients?

2. How do you choose a restaurant?

3. How can you combine entertainment with business communication?

Part Three Reading Task

Reading Task One

You are required to examine the following case and analyze from the perspective of different cultural backgrounds as well as source and retrieval of information the reason why Anson refused to cooperate with Lin Kai's company.

A Case Study on Business Etiquette

A communication starts from a source of information and ends in the retrieval of information. In a social situation, the participants can play both roles of the source and the retrieval of information and they can also interpret the other side's message in their own way. It means the utterance meaning of the source may not be fully taken as the source side expected.

For example, Mr. Anson, a German, partner of Lin Kai's organization, came to Chongqing, the base of Lin Kai's organization, to make an evaluation before signing an agreement which might bring about a sum of investment to replace the old equipment of the production line in Lin Kai's company. Lin Kai held an expensive (luxurious) welcoming party for Mr. Anson. Let's see what happened at the dinner:

Lin Kai: Just a small meal to welcome your visit. Help yourself, please.

Anson: I think it's a banquet, and every dish is so amazing. I enjoy them very much but I'm afraid it is too much for us.

Lin Kai: Oh, this is nothing. It is just a few dishes and a little plain wine, and I'm afraid it can't fully express our respect and good wishes. If we have more chances in future, we'll make better arrangements to make you more pleased and satisfied.

After dinner, Anson wrote a memo to his company that Lin Kai's is not an adequate partner as its management is not very much practical in business, for「they look more willing to invest into their dinner than their production line」.

Question:

Why did Anson refuse to cooperate with Lin Kai's company?

_____

_____

_____

_____

_____

_____

Reading Task Two

Read the passage and choose the right answers.

Manners in every country are different. What is polite in China may not be polite in the United States. These basic rules will help you enjoy western food with your American friends.

Always put the napkin on your lap first. Before you leave the table, fold your napkin and put it beside your plate.

As the meal is served, use the silverware farthest from the plate first. When eating something in a bowl, do not leave the spoon in the bowl. Put it on the plate beneath the bowl. Soup, as well as all American food is eaten quietly. Do not slurp the soup. The soup spoon is used by moving the spoon away from you. Do not overfill the spoon. The bowl may be tipped slightly away from you to allow the last bit of soup to be collected on the spoon. Do not pick the bowl up to hold it closer to your mouth. When you have finished your meal, place your knife and fork side by side on the plate. This signals that you have finished eating.

Wait until everyone has been served to begin eating. Everyone begins to eat at the same time. The host or hostess may invite you to start eating before everyone is served. Some foods may be cold if you are required to wait until everyone is served. If invited to begin before others are served, wait until three or four people have been served before starting to eat.

While eating, remember not to talk with your mouth full of food. During the meal, the host or hostess will offer you a second helping of food. Sometimes they will ask you to help yourself. When they offer you food, give a direct answer. If you refuse the first time, they might not ask you again.

At the table, ask others to pass you dishes that are out of your reach. Good phrases to know are:「Please pass the ＿＿＿＿」or「Could you hand me the ＿＿＿＿, please?」If asked to pass the salt to someone, you should pass both the salt and pepper which are placed on the table together. Hand the salt and pepper to the person seated next to you. Do not reach over the person next to you to pass anything to others.

Sit up straight at the table. Bring the food up to your mouth. Do not lean down to your plate.

Cut large pieces of meat, potatoes and vegetables into bite size pieces. Eat the pieces one at a time.

When eating spaghetti, wind the noodles up on your fork. You may use your spoon to assist in winding the noodle on your fork. The spaghetti on your fork should be eaten in one bite. It is very impolite to eat half your noodles and allow the other half to fall back on your plate.

Some foods may be eaten with your fingers. If you are not sure if it is proper to eat something by picking it up with your fingers, watch what others do before doing so yourself. Examples of foods which can be eaten with your fingers include: bacon which has been cooked until it is very crisp; bread should be broken rather than cut with a knife; cookies; sandwiches; and small fruits and berries on the stem. Most fast foods are intended to be eaten with your fingers.

Do not lean on your arm or elbow while eating. You may rest your hand and wrist on the edge of the table.

In America, people do not use toothpicks at the table.

Some of the rules mentioned here may be somewhat relaxed in informal settings.

The best way to learn good manners is to watch others. Observe the way your western friends eat. This is the best way to avoid making mistakes when you are unsure of what to do.

Questions:

1. Which of the following table manners is inappropriate?

A) When the meal is served, use the silverware nearest from the plate first.

B) When eating spaghetti, use the spoon to assist in winding the noodle on your fork.

C) Cut large pieces of meat, potatoes and vegetables into bite size pieces.

D) Hand the salt and pepper someone wants to the person seated next to you.

2. Which of the following foods can NOT be eaten with your fingers?

A) Sandwiches.　　B) Cookies.　　C) All fast foods.　　D) Berries on the stem.

3. What are the things you can't do during a meal?

A) Lean on your arm or elbow while eating.

B) When eating something in a bowl, leave the spoon in the bowl.

C) Eat half your noodles and allow the other half to fall back on your plate when eating spaghetti.

D) All of the above.

Part Four　Supplementary Materials

Useful Expressions: Eight Regional Cuisines & Tastes in China

Shandong Cuisine	山东菜系（鲁菜）
Taste: fresh (鲜), crisp (脆), tender (软), not greasy (不腻)	
Sichuan Cuisine	四川菜系（川菜）
Taste: spicy and pungent (香辣), tongue-numbing (麻)	

Guangdong Cuisine	廣東菜系（粵菜）
Taste：clear（清），light（淡），crisp（脆），fresh（鮮）	
Fujian Cuisine	福建菜系（閩菜）
Taste：sweet（甜），sour（酸），salty（咸），savory（香）	
Jiangsu Cuisine	江蘇菜系（蘇菜）
Taste：light（淡），fresh（鮮），sweet（甜），with delicate elegance（雅）	
Anhui Cuisine	安徽菜系（徽菜）
Taste：salty（咸），spicy（辣），heavy（味重），braising and stewing（燜炖）	
Zhejiang Cuisine	浙江菜系（浙菜）
Taste：tender（嫩），fresh（鮮），smooth（滑），with mellow fragrance（香）	
Hunan Cuisine	湖南菜系（湘菜）
Taste：thick and pungent（極辣），sour（酸）	

Useful Sentences：Placing & Taking Orders

1. May I take your order, please?
2. What do you recommend?
3. What's your specialty?
4. Anything to drink?
5. Of course, I'll be back with it.
6. How do you like the food?
7. Your food is perfect combination of color, shape, appearance and flavor.
8. Please bring me the bill, Miss.
9. Can I pay by traveler's check/ credit card/ cash/ transfer?
10. It's my treat. / Let's go Dutch.

Skill: Translation of Chinese Dishes

1. 以烹制方法開頭的菜名翻譯方法
   公式：烹法+主料（形狀/口感）
        烹法+主料（形狀/口感）+ with + 輔料
        烹法+主料（形狀/口感）+ with / in + 味汁
e. g.
   roast duck（烤鴨）; grilled lamb chop（烤羊排）; barbecued chicken leg（烤雞腿）; steamed bread（饅頭）; stewed beef（紅燴牛肉）; deep-fried crispy chicken breast（酥炸雞胸）; pan-fried flatfish（煎比目魚）; stir-fried cabbage（清炒大白菜）

2. 以口感開頭的菜名翻譯方法
   公式：口感+主料
        口感+主料 + with + 輔料
e. g.
   crispy beef filet（酥皮牛柳）; smoked salmon（腌熏三文魚）; salted duck eggs（咸鴨蛋）; preserved eggs（皮蛋）

Part Five Assignment

Translate the Chinese dishes into English version.

咸鴨蛋 _____   皮蛋 _____

煎蛋 _____   脆皮乳鴿 _____

皮蛋豆腐 _____   臘肉炒香芹 _____

青椒肉絲 _____   豉汁蒸排骨 _____

牛肉炖土豆 _____   韭菜炒雞蛋 _____

紅燒甲魚＿＿＿＿＿＿＿＿＿＿＿＿　　　　香辣蟹＿＿＿＿＿＿＿＿＿＿＿＿

Unit Eleven   Marketing & Sales

Objectives

Students are able to:

- understand the basic types of advertising and sales promotion;
- comprehend the basic definition of marketing strategy;
- understand basic stages of a typical sales interview;
- grasp words and expressions in marketing and sales;
- conduct marketing and sales interviews.

Part One　Listening Task

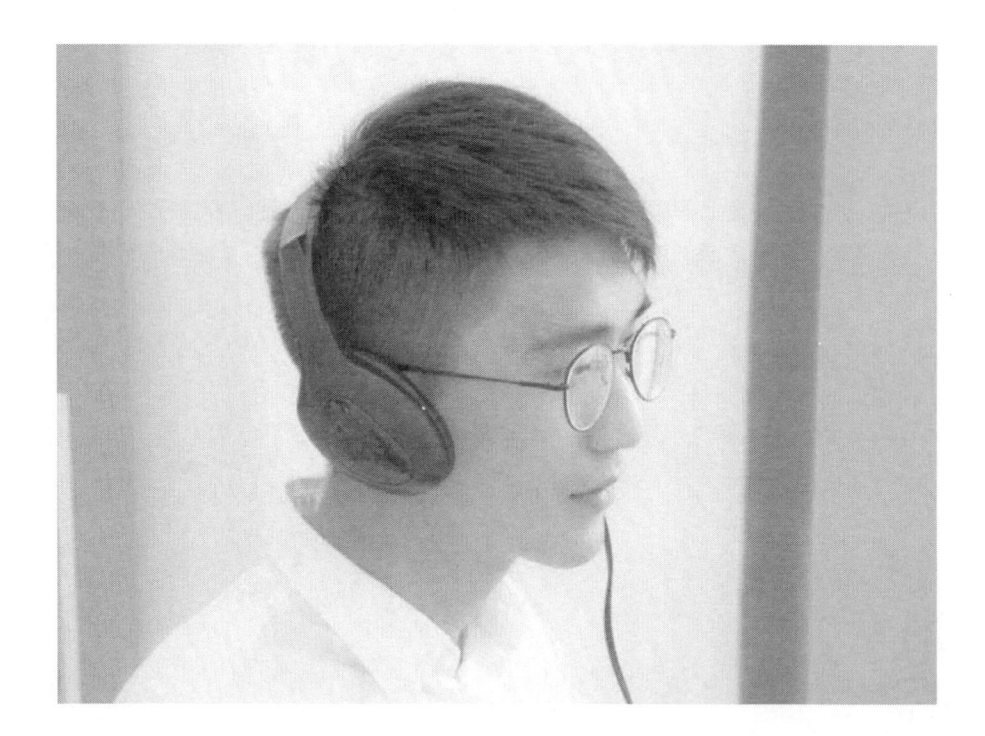

Listening Task One

Listen to a short passage about market research data collection techniques and fill in the blanks.

　　There are two ways of getting as much as possible about potential customers and possible competition from other companies when we set out to market a new product. The first is through primary research and this (1) _____ getting out there and talking to people. We prepare a questionnaire that considers the likes, dislikes, and (2) _____ of consumers, and we try to find out what newspapers and (3) _____ they read. This information can also be gathered (4) _____ a phone interview. We can also make note of what shoppers buy when they

go out as well as using television panels where consumers and retailers give (5) _____.
The other type of research requires (6) _____ physical effort and is often referred to as (7) _____ research. Sales reports and trade figures are (8) _____ for existing information. Magazines, newspapers, and government (9) _____ as well as Internet searches provide useful data. So let's consider some of these in more (10) _____.

Listening Task Two

Listen to a short passage about what makes a good salesperson and tick (√) the points that are mentioned and cross (×) the points that are not mentioned.

(   ) 1. Pick up on a person's personality traits.

(   ) 2. When extremely busy, make an automated answering machine get your phone calls.

(   ) 3. Create an emotional link with the customer.

(   ) 4. Deal with complaints head on.

(   ) 5. Recognize indecisiveness and help customers make a decision.

(   ) 6. Like people and recognize their needs and wants.

(   ) 7. Show customers what they are asking for.

(   ) 8. Be a good listener.

(   ) 9. Sell products that you like.

(   ) 10. The word「try」should not be in a good sales person's vocabulary.

Part Two　Speaking Task

Brainstorm:

Questions for Discussion

　　1. Could you please name several products (goods and services) that are produced or provided in your city or region? How strongly or weakly is each of them marketed?

　　2. Discuss with your groups and match the following terms on consumer sales promotion in Column A with their respective descriptions in Column B.

Column A	Column B
1) special offer	a. something the customer is given, usually by a company, without having to pay for it
2) loyalty card	b. a product, service or program that is offered at reduced prices or rates
3) bonus pack deal	c. a plastic card that some shops give to regular customers. Each time the customer buys something from the shop, points are electronically stored on their card and can be exchanged later for goods or services
4) coupon	d. The packaging offers a consumer a certain percentage more of the product for the same price.
5) loss leader	e. a piece of printed paper which allows you to pay less money than usual for a product, or to get it free

Column A	Column B
6) free-standing insert (FSI)	f. Consumers get one sample for free. After their trial they could decide whether to buy or not.
7) sampling	g. a coupon booklet that is inserted into the local newspaper or magazine for delivery
8) freebie	h. an item that is sold at such a low price that it makes a loss in the hope that customers will be attracted by it and buy other goods at the same shop

3. Advertising through different media can cover nearly every corner of the world. The main channels of it include TV, radio, the Internet, newspapers, billboards, posters and magazines. What are their respective advantages and disadvantages?

Part Three Reading Task

Reading Task One

Read the following passage and decide whether the following statements are true or false. Write (T) for true and (F) for false.

Marketing Strategy

Marketing strategy is the process of planning and implementing company policies towards realizing company goals in accordance with the company vision. Marketing strategies can be identified by the goals they attempt to accomplish in order to boost company profits.

The three basic marketing strategies include price reduction (for market share growth), product differentiation, and market segmentation. The market share strategy calls for reducing production costs in order to reduce consumer prices. Via this strategy, companies strive to manufacture products inexpensively and efficiently and thereby capture a greater share of the market. The product differentiation strategy involves distinguishing a company's products from its competitors' by modifying the image or the physical characteristics of the products. Unlike the market share strategy, product differentiation requires raising product prices to increase profit margins. Companies adopting this strategy hope that consumers will pay higher prices for superior products. Market segmentation refers to the process of breaking the entire market into a series of smaller markets based on common characteristics related to consumer behavior. Once the market is divided into smaller segments, companies can launch marketing programs to cater to the needs and preferences of the individual segments.

Questions:

(　) 1. Four marketing strategies are mentioned in the passage in order to realize the company goals.

(　) 2. Via price reduction strategy, it's possible for the company to capture greater share of market.

(　) 3. Both price reduction strategy and production differentiation strategy require raising product prices to increase profit margins.

(　) 4. Market segmentation divides the whole market into several smaller ones according to the characteristics of customers' behavior.

(　) 5. The marketing programs carried out by companies should cater to the needs and preferences of the individual segments.

Reading Task Two

Read the following passage and choose the right answers.

If we look at a typical sales interview where you meet a client or where a salesperson visits you to sell you something, we see that there are three stages: the Opening Stage, the Building Stage and the Closing Stage.

The first stage is usually a phone call. But you might be preceding it with a letter, or a brochure or something like that. The first thing you have to do is to get past the secretary, which is the most important. Find out when exactly you can talk to your prospective customer. Don't accept a promise to ring you back. And you need to explain who you are and what you're selling. And arrange an appointment.

And the second is what we call the Building Stage, in other words, the sales interview itself. It's important to prepare well and rehearse doing this sales interview. And you can role-play it with a friend or a relation who should try to be unfriendly and uncooperative and difficult, to give you the right sort of practice. Then dress suitably for the occasion. Behave in a friendly, confident but businesslike manner. And remember not to spend too long on social conversation, for it makes people impatient before getting down to business. And remember that your client is a busy person. So respect that. Try and show the client that you're a responsible, trustworthy person, which of course you are.

Tell the client about all the other well-known firms who use your product. Let the client know the benefits of the product. But be careful that you don't do all the talking. Ask him open questions instead of ones he can just answer with a yes or no, to find out what his needs are, so that you can match your product to those needs and to find out how large and how frequent an order he may place. And you should talk only about half the time.

And finally you get to stage three: the Closing Stage – recognizing that your client wants to buy and is on the point of confirming that order. Now this is the hardest part, because it depends on timing. You have to judge when your client is ready to place that order. Then you can thank him for the order and go on to your next appointment.

Questions:

1. What would be the best title of this passage?

A) Job Interview   B) Sales Interview

C) Television Interview   D) Appraisal Interview

2. Which of the following stages is not involved in the process of selling products?

A) Opening Stage.   B) Building Stage.

C) Closing Stage.   D) Transaction Stage.

3. In the first stage of sales, what should be avoided?

A) It is important to get past the secretary.

B) Do explain who you are and what you are selling.

C) Leave your name card and wait for the prospective customer ringing you back.

D) Remember to arrange an appointment.

4. The second stage involves all the following behaviors except _____.

A) Be well-prepared and rehearse with a friend who should try to be uncooperative

B) Dress suitably for the occasion

C) Before getting down to business, try to have a long social conversation so as to develop a friendly relationship with your clients

D) Try to show the clients that you are responsible and trustworthy

5. Which of the following statement is true?

A) Don't mention other well-known firms who use your product.

B) Tell the clients the advantages and disadvantages of your product.

C) A prospective client will tell you the exact time when he is ready to place an order.

D) Encourage your client to talk by asking open questions and only talk half the time yourself.

Part Four Supplementary Materials

Useful Expressions: Marketing & Sales

marketing network	行銷網路	pricing strategy	定價策略
production concept	生產觀念	brand strategy	品牌策略
cash discount	現金折扣	seasonal discount	季節折扣
distribution channel	分銷渠道	exclusive distribution	獨家分銷
wholesaler	批發商	retailer	零售商
convenience store	便利店	discount store	折扣店
marketing research	市場調研	marketing concept	行銷理念
target audience	目標受眾	target market	目標市場
trial sale	試銷	sales slip/receipt	小票/收據
best seller	暢銷品	in stock	現貨
selling point	賣點	out of stock	缺貨
after-sales service	售后服務	word of mouth	口碑
hard sell	強行推銷	bottom price	底價
warranty/guarantee	保修單	refund/rebate	退款

Useful Sentences: Promotion

1. This product has been a best seller for nearly one year.

2. First of all, I will outline the features of our product.

3. The distinction of our product is its light weight.

4. I strongly recommend this product.

5. I think you have to acknowledge that this feature will appeal to many users of microwaves in the West.

6. I assure you that it is a good bargain.

7. How about taking a look at our latest products in our showroom?

8. Our T-shirts have found a ready market in the eastern part of China.

9. Chinese slippers are very popular in your market on account of their superior quality and competitive price.

10. It's on sale at the moment.

Part Five　Assignment

If you are given a chance to introduce a product you are familiar with to its prospective customers, which product would you like to choose? Make promotions for your chosen product using any resources available, such as PowerPoint, etc.

Unit Twelve   Financial Matters

Objectives

Students are able to:

- know the importance and purpose of financing;
- read some comparatively simple reports about financial matters and grasp the main ideas;
- acquire some useful expressions and financial terms;
- introduce some financial products to others.

Part One　Listening Task

Listening Task One

Listen to the recording and finish the following exercise. Complete the following blanks with the information you hear.

Fixed Assets	
Buildings	400, 000
Equipment	_____
Motor Vehicles	_____
Total	510, 000

Current Assets	
Stock	————
Cash	2,000
Trade debtor	————
Total	14,000
Current Liabilities	
Bank overdraft	————
Trade creditors	800
Total	3,300

Listening Task Two

Listen to a conversation about various types of investment and match the advantages and disadvantages with the corresponding investment types with the information you hear.

Advantages:

Stocks and shares	high returns possible; relatively safe – property holds value; can borrow against value of property
Bonds	make a lot of money quickly
Fixed-interest investments	chance of making large profits
Property	low levels of risk
Index futures	guaranteed the return of your money along with promised interest payments – no risk

Disadvantages:

Stocks and shares	need to be well informed; depend on ability to predict direction of demand

Bonds	returns are low; investment generally tied in
Fixed-interest investments	can lose all your money including the principal
Property	cost of maintenance
Index futures	cannot make a lot of money

Part Two Speaking Task

Brainstorm:

Questions for Discussion

1. In the conversation you've just heard, there are some different options for investing money, such as stocks, bonds and property. Which one(s) would you like to choose? Or do you have other suggestions? Please give the reasons.

2. List the expenses that students have to pay when they are away at college. Calculate your total expenses and compare with your classmates.

3. Do you think financial management is important for people or companies? Why or why not?

Part Three Reading Task

Reading Task One

Read the following passage and decide whether the following statements are true or false. Write (T) for true and (F) for false.

Itsbuzzin. Com was created in 1998 to sell fashion clothing over the Internet. By the time the company was liquidated in May 2000, huge amounts of capital had been spent on the venture. *The Financial Times* described Itsbuzzin. Com as 「Europe's first big Internet casualty」.

What went wrong? Company founders spent $120 million on start-up and within a few months the company was valued at $380 million. However, bad management decisions led to spiraling costs that brought the company down. Its expected success was based on predictions that online shopping would increase to $20 billion by 2005. Online shopping has increased, but the market analysis for clothing products was not accurate.

But this was not the only problem. The overall financial outlay of Itsbuzzin. Com was too high. Huge investments were made in complex website technology, which then experienced problems that drove costs even higher. The online catalogue was very expensive – it had to be translated into several European languages – and it then needed further expenditure to keep it updated. Large number of staff were hired, resulting in a huge payroll and enormous expense accounts. The company offered free delivery, which created very high postal costs. When items were returned, delivery costs doubled. Itsbuzzin. Com found itself in serious trouble and eventually collapsed. Major shareholders lost vast sums of money, advertising agencies were owed around $ 25 million, and many staff members went unpaid.

Questions:

(　) 1. The Itsbuzzin company started up with $ 380 million.

(　) 2. Market analysis for online fashion wear sales was not realistic.

(　) 3. Itsbuzzin's high operating costs were one of the major causes of its failure.

(　) 4. Advertisers, shareholders and staff were compensated for their losses.

(　) 5. Staff spoke different languages so there were large expense accounts.

(　) 6. Offering free delivery turned out to be a very expensive decision.

Reading Task Two

Read the following passage and choose the right answers.

Five Simple Methods for Good Money Management

If you have found that your finances are getting a bit beyond your control, there are some methods that you can take that will lead to good money management. The following five methods can help get you off to a running start.

Stop Using Credit Cards

Credit cards can be very tempting. They are even more tempting when we are dry on cash and waiting for our next pay day. But those little charges add up quickly and fast. When you only pay the minimum payment due, you get tapped for interest fees quickly, too. A good rule of thumb here is to never, ever use your credit cards. Think along the lines of: if you can't afford to buy it for cash now, then you can't really afford it. Rather, make strides to pay down these cards as much as possible instead of adding to them.

Stop Eating Out

While it certainly may be tempting to go out with your friends, good money management says this is a bad idea. Eating out costs a lot more than eating in. And plenty of us are guilty of eating out too often. A quick look at your bank statement will reveal if you are eating out too much. Go ahead and highlight all of the charges for restaurants and coffee to-go, and you will quickly find that doing something as simple as staying in more often can save you thousands per year.

Know Your Equity

You may have some existing equity that you can use to pay off your debts and roll them into one more feasible monthly payment. If you own your own home or other property, you can consider refinancing it to pull some of the equity out. Mortgage rates are at all times low, and you could qualify to reduce your debt by paying it off with your existing equity for a lower interest long term loan that's far easier to pay off.

Project Your Budget

Knowing what you have coming in versus what you have going out is incremental in you managing your money better. A good place to start is with creating a spreadsheet of all your bills versus incoming funds. This will tell you what you can afford to spend to pay down debt or spend on entertainment so that you don't overspend in the future.

See the Difference

A number of money management apps are out there, plenty of which are free to use. Certain premium features may remain locked on a few of these 15 money management apps listed by Life Hack. But they all still have decent functionality in the free versions. More importantly, they help you better manage your finances by enabling you to visualize where your funds are going so you can get a better grip on how you spend your greenbacks.

Questions:

1. Which of the following is not a disadvantage of using credit cards according to the passage?

A) Little charges add up quickly and fast.

B) When you only pay the minimum payment due, you get tapped for interest fees quickly.

C) Credit cards will help you get through really hard periods when you lack money.

D) Using credit cards may tempt you to buy things you can't really afford.

2. Which of the following statements is NOT true according to the passage?

A) Eating out is always a bad idea.

B) Eating out costs a lot more than eating in.

C) It is sometimes a good idea to reduce your debt by paying it off with your existing equity.

D) A good budget will help you kill overspending in the future.

3. What are the advantages of money management apps?

A) Plenty of them are free.

B) They help you better manage your finances by enabling you to visualize where your funds are going.

C) They enable you to get a better grip on how you spend your greenbacks.

D) All of the above.

Part Four Supplementary Materials

Useful Expressions: Investment

portfolio	投資組合	liquidity	資產折現力
valuation	股價	fixed-interest investment	固定利息投資
equity funds	股票型基金	annual rate of interest	年利率
handling charge	手續費	interest	利息
net profit	純利潤	gross profit	毛利潤
bid price	買入價	offer price	賣出價
list price	標價；建議售價	investment adviser	投資顧問
tangible/physical assets	有形資產	diversification	分散投資
inflation	通貨膨脹	deflation	通貨緊縮
overdraw	透支	devaluation	貶值
dividend	紅利	foreign exchange	外匯
deposit book	存折	go bankrupt	破產
on the hook	被套住	pay-in slip	存款單

Useful Sentences: Introducing a Financial Product

1. If you don't finance, you will have no finances.

2. In recent years, structured financing products are developing fast, and becoming more and more popular in our country.

3. You had better put some of your money into an annuity for safety reasons.

4. Annuity proceeds bypass probate and goes directly to the beneficiary listed on the beneficiary form.

5. Here's a story that may help retain my recommendation.

6. While you can buy a basic estate planning package online, it's always a good idea to have a professional who could make sure your forms, directives, and trusts are correctly executed.

7. As your circumstances change, your estate plan needs to grow and adapt as well.

8. This is an offer with mutual benefits. There's a good chance that in five years you could be a successful entrepreneur running your own business.

9. We want to invite you to join us now with this great special offer.

10. Our financial product will bring you highest proceeds but lowest risk.

Part Five Assignment

Investigate more about at least one concrete financial product (*e. g. zhaocaibao*) and share it with the whole class. (You can read newspapers, surf the Internet or ask your parents or friends).

Appendix: Keys and Tape Scripts

Unit One Making Your Career Choices

Part One Listening Task

(T) 1. Consulting with different businesses and finding out what is required in each department are helpful when we are making decisions on the future job.

(F) 2. There are not many career choices for the students who major in Business.

(T) 3. Job hunters should also look at some ads and see what is available in the real world.

(T) 4. When we are making decisions about what we want to do, we can start by thinking about our specific interests in business.

(F) 5. A job in Human Resources or Management would probably suit John.

(T) 6. We, the job hunters, are supposed to identify our own strengths and weaknesses in each area.

(T) 7. For graduates, it's advisable to visit college counselors.

Tape Script

Martha: I think it's time we started thinking about our future and making decisions about what we want to do when we finish this course.

John: Oh, Martha, you're always so serious! We still have two months before we take our final exams.

Martha: I know, but you can't just suddenly wake up the day you finish college and find a job. You need to plan.

John: You're right, of course. But where do we start? The course we're taking is General Business and there are so many choices like Human Resources, Sales, Marketing, Finance, and so on. And I'm not even sure what I'm interested in.

Martha: Yes, I know. There's a lot to think about, but maybe we can start by thinking about our specific interests in Business. For example, I think that you should go into Marketing.

John: I've thought about that too, but I'm not sure. I suppose we should think about our different strengths and weaknesses in each area. A job in Human Resources or Management would probably suit you. You are bossy – you just love telling people what to do!

Martha: Hey, that's not true. It's just that I like organizing people and I think I'm pretty good at it.

John: Well, build on your strengths. I think we should also have a look at some ads and find out what kinds of jobs are out there in the real world.

Martha: Okay. Let's buy the newspaper every day this week and look at job ads in Business. We could also go to some companies and find out what skills and qualifications are needed for each department.

John: Good plan. I think maybe we should go to see our college counselor too. She may have some useful advice for us.

Martha: Let's do that. I'll call her office tomorrow and see when we can get an appointment. I'll arrange for both of us to see her.

John: Great! I've got to hurry. I have a class in ten minutes. Bye.

Martha: Okay. See you later.

Part Three　Reading Task

Reading Task One

1. Proficiency in MS office, good interpersonal skills, and good telephone manners.

2. Responsibility for a number of key existing accounts and the development of new business.

3. Salary.

4. No, but it is preferable.

5. The on-the-job training and the commission on car sales.

Reading Task Two

1-4: BDAC

Unit Two　Resume

Part One　Listening Task

Listening Task One

(√) address　　　　　　(√) experience

(×) age　　　　　　　　(√) interests

(√) all your education　　(×) marital status

(√) consenting references　(×) religion

(√) e-mail　　　　　　　(√) volunteer work

Tape Script

HR Manager: Your resume is a very important document and with your application and cover letter it's the employer's first introduction to you, and the measure of your suitability for the job. Remember that employers receive a lot of applications, so you have to make all your documents as readable and as user-friendly as possible.

The layout of your resume should be in a simple font, 11 or 12 point in Times New Roman or Arial script. Your contact details should be up-to-date and the e-mail address serious and not too much of an attention-grabber.

We generally advise people not to include age and marital status because some people object to being asked these questions. Likewise, you don't have to include information about your religion though sometimes this question may appear on the application form. It's advisable to include all information about your work experience, including temporary and part-time jobs since this will give the employer some insight into your background in dealing with customers and working as part of a team. Of course, give all relevant information about your education and include details on your involvement in sports and volunteer work, too, because this shows your personality. Of course, you should read the job ad carefully and follow the instructions given there. Make sure that you get approval from your references before including their names on your resume.

Listening Task Two

Jane was (1) impressed by both Applicant 1 and Applicant 2 for different reasons. Applicant 1 has quite a lot of experience - over (2) 20 years, but he is a little short in (3) academic qualifications. Applicant 2 has an M. A. in HR as well as a General Business degree, but on the experience side she is a little (4) weak. However, Applicant 1 has had wide range of (5) responsibilities in very important HR areas at (6) management levels. As the company is looking for someone who's a (7) team player and that's probably easier for a person who's (8) new in the (9) workplace. Both applicants will be (10) invited for an interview.

Tape Script

Manager: Jane, what was your overall impression of the applicants?

Jane: I was impressed with both, but for very different reasons.

Manager: Yes, I agree. Applicant 1 has quite a lot of experience - overall 20 years, but is a little short in academic qualifications.

Jane: Yes, that's true whereas Applicant 2 has an M. A. in HR, and a very recent one, as well as a General Business degree. It's very important to have up-to-date theoretical knowledge.

Manager: You're right about that, but on the experience side don't you think she's a little weak?

Jane: Of course, but she's worked at that mortgage company, which has given her some experience on the financial side of things whereas Applicant 1 has had more experience, but in more general situations.

Manager: True, but look at the wide range of responsibilities he's had in very important HR areas at management levels.

Jane: But we're looking for someone who's a team player and that's probably easier for a person who's new in the workplace. I wonder about the flexibility of a person who's been in management for so long.

Manager: Let's invite them both for an interview and keep these questions in mind as we're interviewing.

Jane: Good plan. I'll call them and make arrangements.

Part Three Reading Task

Reading Task One
Possible answers:

✓ To be a teacher of the 21st century, a good command of English or linguistic competence is not enough.

✓ There are a variety of elements that contribute to the qualities of a good English teacher. These elements can be categorized into 3 groups: ethic devotion, professional qualities and personal styles.

✓ A good English teacher should be resourceful, well-informed, professionally trained and creative.

Reading Task Two

1. Because their education experience is more relevant.

2. In skeletal form.

3. If they were your highest educational qualification or they were particularly good.

4. Most recent first (in reverse chronological order).

5. Add an additional relevant section on IT skills.

Unit Three Application Letters

Part One   Listening Task

John: John is really good at (1) <u>networking</u> and has a way with people that would be very good in sales and (2) <u>marketing</u>. As for the weaknesses, he is a bit (3) <u>lazy</u> about getting himself moving. But it's not a good idea to tell a (4) <u>prospective</u> employer that he is lazy, so he is advised to say he is considered a bit (5) <u>disorganized</u>, and he is working on his organizational skills.

Martha: Martha's skills are (6) <u>organizational</u>. She is good at planning and seeing things (7) <u>through</u>. Some people would say that she is (8) <u>impatient</u>, but this may be because she has a lot of drive and (9) <u>enthusiasm</u> to get the job done. She can organize herself and (10) <u>check</u> everything as she goes along.

Tape Script

Martha: John, remember Mrs. Mills talked about strengths and weaknesses? I have seen those on the applications and find it really hard to look at myself and decide what my strengths and weaknesses are.

John: I know, my brother said it's a matter of finding the balance between selling yourself and what you are good at, but not making yourself sound perfect. In other words, you need to be a bit critical of yourself without overdoing it. OK, so let's think and help each other out.

Martha: Well, John, I think you are really good at networking. You have a way with people and making contacts that I think would be very good in sales and marketing.

John: Wow, thanks, Martha. As for you, I think your skills are organizational. You are very good at planning and seeing things through. This is definitely one of my weak areas. I think I'm just a bit lazy about getting myself moving.

Martha: Well, John, I don't think it's a good idea to tell a prospective employer that you're lazy. You can't completely hide the negative, but you need to put it in a more positive way. How about saying that you might be considered a bit disorganized, but that's because you focus on the communication side of the task and you're working on your organizational skills. As for myself, I could say that some people might say that I'm impatient, but this may be because I have a lot of drive and enthusiasm to get the job done. I still organize myself and check everything as I go along.

Part Three Reading Task

Reading Task One

1. Polite.

2. It must display for what purpose you are asking the loan and how you have planned to repay it.

3. If you are applying for a leave, write the period of leave you wish to take and the reason for the same in a few words.

4. You can close the letter with a phrase like thanking you, yours truly, sincerely yours, etc.

5. A good-quality paper is super white, crisp, and of A4 size.

Reading Task Two

1-5: BCBCD

Unit Four Job Interviews

Part One   Listening Task

Listening Task One

Possible answers:

✓ In the summers of 1997 and 1998, I worked as a sales girl for P&G in Guangzhou. (work experience)

✓ I have a Bachelor's Degree in Business Administration. (qualifications)

✓ I passed TEM-8 at college and I am good at oral English. (skills)

✓ Two years ago I was appointed as Brand Manager, responsible for the Panda line of biscuits. (achievements)

Tape Script

Mary: May I come in?

Harry: Yes, please do.

Mary: Good morning, Sir. My name is Mary Wang. I've come for an interview as you requested.

Harry: Nice to meet you, Miss Wang. I am Harry White, the Director of the HR Department. I was expecting you. Please take a seat.

Mary: Thank you.

Harry: Well, Miss Wang, you're applying for the position of Sales Manager, right? How did you know about our company?

Mary: I got to know the name of P&G from such famous Brands as Rejoice 2&1, Head & Shoulders and Pantene. Also, in the summers of 1997 and 1998, I worked as a sales girl for P&G in Guangzhou.

Harry: Really? That's good! Then you must know something about our company.

Mary: Yes, a little. P&G is a famous company. Your cosmetics and skin-care products are very popular with women all over the world.

Harry: That's right. Miss Wang, can you tell me which university you attended?

Mary: Sun Yat-Sen.

Harry: And what degree have you got?

Mary: I have a Bachelor's Degree in Business Administration.

Harry: How is your English? You know some staff members in our company are Americans. So conversational English is very important.

Mary: I passed TEM-8 at college and I am good at oral English. I think I can communicate with Americans quite well.

Harry: Good. I know you're now with United Butter. What's your chief responsibility there?

Mary: I worked there for five years ever since I graduated from college. Two years ago I was appointed as Brand Manager, responsible for the Panda line of biscuits.

Harry: Why do you want to change your job?

Mary: Ah, I want to change my working environments, seek new challenges and broaden my experience. That's why I want to move to sales.

Harry: What do you think is the most important qualification for a sales person?

Mary: I think it's self-confidence and quality products.

Harry: I agree with you. What salary would you expect to get here?

Mary: Well, I would leave it to you to decide after you consider my abilities. My current annual income at United Butter is 150,000. But, er, could you tell me a little more about what the job entails.

Harry: You'll be in charge of all the sales activities for all P&G hair products in Northeast China. This would involve market analysis, client service and development, sales promotions and regular customer satisfaction surveys. You'd report directly to the regional Sales Director.

Do you have any other questions?

Mary: Yes, only one. When can I have your decision?

Harry: I need to discuss with other Board Members. We'll notify you of our decision as soon as possible. But, to be honest, you seem to be a good candidate with the right kind of experience and personality. You are high on my list.

Mary: That's good. Thank you, Mr. White. I'll look forward to hearing from you. Goodbye.

Harry: Goodbye.

Listening Task Two

√ Put the interview into perspective.

√ Be clear.

√ Examples.

√ Never assume.

√ Never slag off.

√ Prepare at least three questions.

√ Listen.

√ Don't talk too much.

√ Do your research.

Tape Script

Hi, welcome to Videojug. I'm Rikke Hansen from Career Concierge, and I'm going to show you how to ace that job interview.

Step 1: Put the interview into perspective. Try to think of this as an exchange between two people, rather than a one-way interrogation. You know they have interest in you; you have interest in them. It should be a two-way thing. It's very helpful actually to think of it like first date. You know you want to make sure you show something of your best side, or you also want to make sure it is the right thing for both of you.

Step 2: Be clear. Be absolutely clear about why they should hire you. You know what are your unique selling points, and how you can match that to what they are looking for. Think about that upfront and really give examples throughout the interview, as to show just how good you are and how relevant your experience is. It's up to you to show them that you are the right candidate for the following reasons. So take every opportunity to get your selling points across.

Step 3: Give examples. Examples, examples, examples. An example is a proof. It's a proof that you have already done what the interview is asking for and you can do it for them again. So really, throughout the interview, give as many examples as you can, and think about it in the following way. Each example should illustrate what was the problem, what you did and what was the result. The great thing about using examples is it helps you avoid clichés, or answering the questions that everybody else would. Your experience and your example is unique, and by giving them examples, you would really stand out as a unique candidate.

Step 4: Never assume. Never assume that the interviewer has read your C. V. So feel free to, you know, talk about things in the C. V., elaborate on them, expanding them, using some examples in there. On the other hand, make sure you know your C. V. as well. There is nothing worse than saying: ⌈Ah, I've already put that in my C. V.⌋

Step 5: Never slag off. Don't ever slag off any formal employees, products, colleagues or experiences. Be very positive by your experience so far.

Step 6: Prepare at least 3 questions. Prepare at least 3 personal questions to actually ask them. Think about what you really want to know. Do you want to know about their management style? The culture of the company? What's important for you to know? And have them prepared, exactly what you are going to ask.

Step 7: Listen. Listen, and read between the lines as to what they really are asking. If you have any doubt, ask them to clarify. But listen, and answer the question asked.

Step 8: Don't talk too much. Don't talk too much or go to excessive details. You know, keep it brief, and keep it succinct and answer the question. If they want more detail, they will ask you. On the other hand, don't just sit like a lemon, and give very short answers. It's the most straining thing for the interviewer. So do engage in conversation.

Step 9: Do your research. Know the company. Research, research, research. Make sure you've done your research before the interview, so you know all the things that are relevant about the company. And make sure that throughout the interview, you bring about a little bits about their products, their competitors to show them that yes, you really know what they are all about.

Part Three Reading Task

Reading Task One

　　1-3: CAB

Reading Task Two

　　1. Interviewer and interviewee.

　　2. She worked in an executive branch as a secretary.

　　3. She was hoping to get an offer of a better position.

　　4. As long as she can continue to learn and to grow in her field.

　　5. The starting salary is not very high, but the fringe benefits are much more. The salary will be raised in a short time if she does well.

Unit Five Company Introduction & Visiting Cards

Part One Listening Task

　　(T) 1. The company was owned by the state.

　　(F) 2. Their registered capital was 5 million *yuan* in 1983.

　　(T) 3. They import and export commodities popular in the global market.

　　(F) 4. Their olive oil is imported from European countries.

　　(T) 5. More than half of their employees have a Master's degree or above.

Tape Script

　　A: Could you tell me something about your corporation?

B: Of course. Our corporation is a large state-owned enterprise. It was set up in 1983 with a registered capital of 50 million *yuan*.

A: What is your major scope of business?

B: We deal in the import and export of commodities popular in the international market.

A: So what are your main products?

B: Our first product is olive oil. It has been sold well in China and exported to European countries.

A: How many employees do you have?

B: We have 721 employees so far. 54% of them have a Master's degree or above.

A: Great.

B: We have recorded a short film about our corporation. It can give you a more detailed description. May I play it now?

A: Fine.

Part Three   Reading Task

Reading Task One

1. It is one of the first full service investment banks and integrated securities brokerage in China.

2. Five. They are GF Futures Co., Ltd., GF Holdings (Hong Kong) Co., Ltd., GF Xinde Investment Management Co., Ltd., GF Qianhe Investment Co., Ltd. and GF Asset Management (Guangdong) Co., Ltd.

3. Prudent operation and standardized management.

4. Spare no effort in its pursuit of excellence and strive to become a top-notch financial group in China and the Asia-Pacific Region.

Reading Task Two

1-3: CDB

Part Five Assignments

1. Chang'an Automobile, founded in 1862, is the pioneer of China's modern industry. It is affiliated to China South Industries Group Corporation. It has existing assets of 128.1 billion *yuan* and nearly 80 000 employees.

Chang'an Automobile has 11 large bases in Chongqing, Beijing, Shanghai, Jiangsu, Hebei, Zhejiang, etc. and 30 vehicle and engine factories, making an annual capacity of 2.6 million vehicles. Over the years, Chang'an Automobile has confidently maintained its place among the Top 500 industrial enterprises in China.

2. Suppose you become a lawyer five years later, your card may be like:

Chengdu New Century Law Firm	
Qiang Xu	
Barrister	
99 Chunxi Road	Tel: 028-88114979
Chengdu City, Sichuan, 600517	
P. R. C.	Fax: 028-88114878
E-mail: xuqiang@263.net	Mobile Phone: 1368329428

Unit Six Memos & Minutes

Part One Listening Task

1. The meeting was postponed.

2. He didn't read the memo.

3. It will help one know what he is missing out on.

Tape Script

M: I have been waiting here in the conference room for ten minutes already. What time does our meeting start? Where is everyone anyway?

W: Didn't you hear about that our meeting was postponed until Friday.

M: What? The meeting was postponed? No one told me anything about it.

W: Didn't you get the memo?

M: What memo? There haven't been any memos this whole week. I check my inbox every day. And I haven't seen anything.

W: The memo went out 3 days ago. It should have been made to your inbox, but maybe it got lost in all the clutter on your desk.

M: You know how things get piled up on my desk when I'm busy. I know that sometimes I do misplace things, but I always read all the memos that go around. They go directly to my inbox. Are you sure it was sent to the whole office?

W: It should have gone around to everybody. They also posted a copy of the memo in the break room. Don't you ever look at the messages posted on the bulletin board?

M: I'm usually too busy to take a bunch of coffee breaks and gossip by the water cooler. Anyway, I'm sure the memo never got to my inbox. I'll have to talk to our secretary about it.

W: That's right. You never know what you are missing out on if you don't read the memos.

Part Three Reading Task

Reading Task One

1. The date/time, location, attendees, objectives, schedule, note-taker, etc.

2. They will have a meeting at Conference Room A at 10:00 on January15, 2015.

3. The sales manager – John Walker and all the salespersons.

4. Review the sales in the past three months, find out the reasons why our sales suffer a downturn and find the ways to change such a terrible situation.

5. The sales manager – John Walker.

Reading Task Two

(T) 1. It is equally important to know when to have a meeting and when not to.

(F) 2. It is not necessary to prepare pens or paper for everyone.

(T) 3. Attaching the minutes of the previous meeting gives members the chance to bring up anything they do not understand or disagree with.

(F) 4. The attendance book or sheet of paper should be signed at the end of the meeting.

(T) 5. AOB in the meeting minutes stands for Any Other Business.

Part Five Assignment

Model:

Memo

To: Mr. Owen, HR Department

From: Mr. Edward, Planning Department

Date: 10 March, 2007

Subject: A Sales Manager Wanted

    I would like to inform you that our company intends to expand its business in China and thereby is in urgent need of a capable sales manager. The requirements of the applicant are as follows.

    First of all, he or she would be experienced in marketing planning, with at least two years' working experience. Secondly, his or her Mandarin and English should be fluent in listening, speaking as well as writing. Thirdly, and also his or her command of computer operation must be highly proficient. Finally, he or she should be an individual gifted with good interpersonal, report-writing and presentation skills. I do hope we can find a right person.

Unit Seven Business Correspondence

Part One Listening Task

The woman is writing a letter to one of her (1) clients, but she wonders how to get it started, because she does not know the name of the (2) contact person. The man suggests that if it is not (3) personal, the letter could be written like this:

To whom it may (4) concern,

We are very (5) grateful for your continued (6) support. Regarding our new (7) product line, we would like to announce a special price (8) discount. Please find enclosed our (9) customer service survey. Please return the survey without (10) delay /at your earliest (11) convenience.

Yours (12) sincerely/faithfully,
Mary White

Tape Script

A: Can you help me a minute?

B: Sure, what can I do for you?

A: I'm trying to write a letter to one of our clients. But I just don't know exactly what to say. I don't even know how to get it started. I know I should write 「Dear Mr. or Ms.」, but the problem is I don't know the name of the contact person.

B: You can just put Dear Sir or Madam, or if it is not personal, you can write 「To whom it may concern」.

A: OK, So I first thank them for their business. I can say something like 「We are very grateful for your continued support.」 How is that?

B: Good! But also, right off the bat you want to tell them the reason you are writing; give them a reference.

A: Like「Regarding our new product line, we would like to announce a special price discount.」

B: Right, do you need them to respond?

A: Yes, the letter would have a survey inside, and they should complete it and return to our office. How should I write that?

B: You can tell them「Please find enclosed our customer service survey」, or also, you can say:「Attached is our customer survey.」If you need the results right away, you can tell them it is urgent by saying「Please return the survey without delay」or「as soon as possible」. Maybe a more polite way is「at your earliest convenience」.

B: Great! And what do you think I should close it with?

A: Since you don't know them that well personally, probably the best way would be「Yours faithfully」or「sincerely」, you could also say「Best regards」. But I don't think that would be appropriate because you don't have the name, and obviously, haven't met them.

B: OK. Thanks a lot for your help!

Part Three　Reading Task

Reading Task One

1. A good business letter is polite, straightforward and brief.

2. It is often judged on small but important things such as format, grammar, punctuation, openings and closings.

3. It is not only critical to the success of our message, but also to the image we wish to present.

4. A well-written business letter can increase your image with prospective and presented clients, and thus build trust and confidence on a company and a brand.

Reading Task Two

(T) 1. Silk blouses in all sizes are needed by ABC Company.

(F) 2. The style of both the letters is modified block style.

(T) 3. Silk blouses for all age groups are produced by PNG Silk Company.

(F) 4. The prices quoted on Quotations Sheet No. 257 include the cost prices and commission for ABC Company.

(T) 5. If ABC Company places an order of US $ 80,000, a quantity discount of 4% will be offered.

Part Five Assignment

執事先生：

多謝5月20日有關第252號訂單的來信。得悉貨物及時運抵，感到高興。

有關第46號箱錯運貨物一事，在此向貴公司致歉。經調查，發現裝運時誤將貨物同放，所以有此錯失。該缺貨已安排即時發運，有關文件準備好后會立即寄出。錯運的貨物煩請代存，本公司已知會代理商，不日將與貴公司聯絡。

因此失誤而引致任何不便，本公司深感歉意。

銷售部主任

托尼·史密斯謹上

Unit Eight Travel for Business

Part One Listening Task

Listening Task One

(×) 1. I will set out to Paris with my assistant.

(√) 2. I booked a round-trip ticket.

(√) 3. I will return on July 21.

Tape Script

A: Hello, can I help you?

B: I want to book an airplane ticket to Paris.

A: When are you going to set out?

B: Next Monday, June 7.

A: We will have tickets on that day.

B: Great.

A: Do you have any idea about when you will come back? It is much cheaper for you to book a round-trip ticket.

B: Yes, a round-trip ticket. I will return on July 21.

A: Fine. I have booked the ticket for you.

B: Thank you.

Listening Task Two

1. She should apply for a business visa to America.

2. She is going to attend a textile exhibition.

3. He asked the woman to show him her invitation letter.

Tape Script

A: Good morning, sir. I'd like to apply for a visa to America.

B: What kind of visa do you want?

A: Business visa.

B: What's the purpose of your American trip?

A: I am invited to attend a textile exhibition.

B: Could you show me your letter of invitation?

A: Certainly. Here you are.

B: Let me have a look at it.

A: How long will it take to get a business visa?

B: We have to spend two weeks to verify all the materials you submitted.

Part Three Reading Task

Reading Task One

1. By showing the references from his four American English teachers about his English and business skills.

2. Yes. He has never broken the law. In addition, he has been studying the laws of the United States so that there will be no problem when he goes there.

3. Two years at the most.

4. To start reading an American newspaper. Try to get a newspaper that is published near his destination. Baltimore, Maryland has a famous paper called *The Baltimore Sun*.

5. About two to three weeks.

Reading Task Two

(F) 1. In China, if you don't greet others with kisses or a warm embrace, you'll be considered cold.

(F) 2. Touching someone on the head who isn't a family member or a good friend in Korea, you'll make them uncomfortable.

(T) 3. In France it is disgusting to blow your nose in public.

(T) 4. Chatting in saunas in Finland is impolite.

(F) 5. Take off your shoes when arriving at the door of a London dinner party and the hostess will find you civilized.

(T) 6. In Morocco, if you eat with your left hand, your fellow diners will feel mortified.

Unit Nine Making Reservations

Part One Listening Task

1. They are possibly customer and hotel receptionist.

2. They are talking about booking/reserving a single room from 15th to 17th this month.

3. Date of arrival, types of room, guest's name, contact number, reservation confirmation.

4. Guest's identity, accept reservation, reservation confirmation, note down necessary information, welcome preparation.

Tape Script

Lindsay: Good afternoon, Wiggins Hotel.

Christopher: Ah, hello, I'm calling to make a reservation for 3 nights, from the fifteenth.

Lindsay: One moment, please ... that's 3 nights, starting on the fifteenth of this month?

Christopher: That's right. A single room.

Lindsay: OK, may I have your name please?

Christopher: Yes. It's Christopher Moreno. That's C-h-r-i-s-t-o-p-h-e-r M-o-r-e-n-o.

Lindsay: OK, Mr. Moreno, that's a single room for 3 nights ... the 15th, 16th, and 17th of this month?

Christopher: Yes, that's right.

Lindsay: Great, and could I have a contact number please?

Christopher: Yes, it's a 070-555-3872.

Lindsay: That's 070-555-3872.

Christopher: Yes, that's right.

Lindsay: OK, thanks. We look forward to seeing you then.

Christopher: OK, thank you.

Part Two Speaking Task

1.

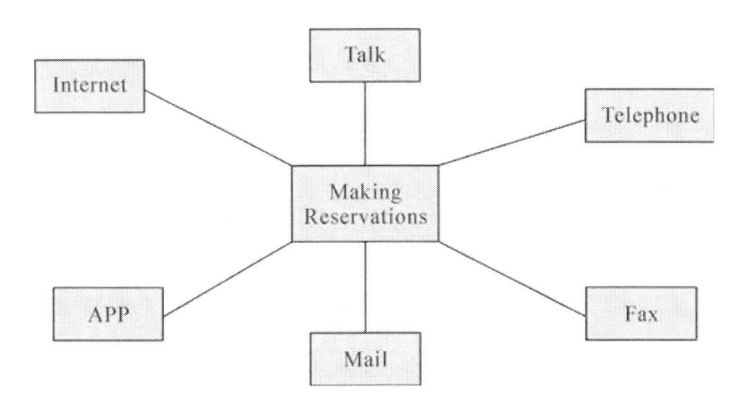

```
         Talk
Internet      Telephone
    Making Reservations
APP           Fax
         Mail
```

2. Match Chinese with English.

Resident Hotel	常住型酒店
Convention Hotel	會議型酒店
Casino Hotel	賭場型酒店
Bed & Breakfast Hotel	家庭式飯店
Motel	汽車旅館
Commercial Hotel	商業型酒店
Resort Hotel	度假型酒店

3. Identify the room types.

standard room / single room / suite

Part Three Reading Task

Reading Task One

1-3: BDC

Reading Task Two

1. People who take vacations that require a hotel stay, or travels for business or their kids' sporting events.

2. Orbitz. Com, Expedia. Com, Travelocity. Com, Hotels. Com, HotelDiscounts. Com, Sidestep. Com and Priceline. Com.

3. High-speed Internet, a refrigerator, a kitchen or kitchenette, and a pull-out sleeper sofa.

4. No.

5. To use the hotel website, rather than a travel site.

Part Five　Assignment

Reservation Form

Hotel Name: Yangtze Island Hotel (Chongqing)

Address: Jiefangbei Pedestrian Street

Tel: 023-60638888

Guest's Name	John Brown, David Smith, Helen Woods and Mary White
Time to check in	4th of November, 2015
Time to check out	6th of November, 2015
Room type and number	two standards with bath and a convention room for 5th of November
Payment	credit card covered by the company
Tel	021-88996263
Fax	021-88996262
E-mail	vivian@163.com

Unit Ten Having Business Dinners

Part One   Listening Task

A: Good morning, Mr. Brown.

B: Good morning. Nice to meet you.

A: Me too. I'm (1) <u>wondering</u> whether you are free on Wednesday night.

B: Let me check my schedule. I don't have an (2) <u>appointment</u> then.

A: Great. I'd like to invite you to have a dinner.

B: It's very kind of you. I have not had Chinese food before.

A: What about Roast Duck? We are planning to hold a banquet in your honor at Quanjude Restaurant.

B: I am (3) <u>delighted</u> to go. I have heard it is famous for its Roast Duck.

A: Exactly. What time would be (4) <u>convenient</u> for you?

B: How about 6 p.m.?

A: OK. I will wait for you at the lounge of the hotel at that time.

B: Fine. Thank you for your invitation.

Having dinner

A: I am (5) <u>glad</u> you have come. Take a seat.

B: Thank you for your (6) <u>entertainment</u>.

A: What would you like to drink? This is world-famous Maotai. Do you want to have a try?

B: No. Thanks. (7) <u>Spirit</u> is too strong for me. Just a glass of red wine.

A: We have just (8) <u>concluded a transaction</u>. Shall we raise a toast to a good cooperation?

B: Cheers. I hope we will have more orders to come.

A: Sure. I would like to propose a toast to (9) the success of business.

B: To our health and friendship.

A: (10) Bottom up.

B: Please make yourself at home.

Part Two   Speaking Task

Speaking Task One

Possible answers:

1.

✓ To secure the loyalty and partnership of the existing/potential clients and gain an advantage over competitors;

✓ To provide rewards or incentives for them;

✓ To provide a relaxed and less formal environment to do business – Mix business with pleasure.

2. We should decide who we are going to entertain, what activities we will do to entertain them and where we will have the entertaining activities.

✓ business dinner: cocktail party

✓ client appreciation banquet

✓ wine tasting & food tasting

✓ concerts or exhibitions

✓ an sightseeing tour of the city

✓ charity events

✓ sporting events

✓ shopping trip

✓ golf …

Speaking Task Two

1. A meal selection has its own time frame.

✓ Breakfasts are great for urgent business.

An English breakfast consists of bacon, eggs, sausage, tomatoes, toast, marmalade, tea, etc.

A continental breakfast consists of breadstuff, toast, croissants, pastries and coffee, tea, or other drinks.

✓ Lunch and supper may last 2 hours.

Serving order: appetizer—soup—main courses—dessert—coffee/tea.

✓ Tea is the new「power meal」. — 4 p. m.

2. How to choose a restaurant:

✓ atmosphere

✓ location

✓ facilities

✓ cleanliness

✓ staff friendliness/ attentiveness

✓ speed of service

✓ quality of food and drink

✓ price of food

Tips on choosing a restaurant:

(1) Select a restaurant that you know well and that your client can find easily.

(2) Choose one restaurant that has top service.

(3) Make sure you have a prime location away from the restroom and the kitchen which allows the client a view of the landscape.

3. How to combine entertainment with business communication:

✓ After watching a football match with your clients, you may invite them to have a meal and discuss business.

✓ Make small talks before you get into any business item.

✓ Start discussing business after the appetizer has been served and do not wait until dessert.

✓ Before the entertaining, invite the guests to your office for a cup of coffee and a boardroom presentation of the new products and services.

✓ After the entertaining activity, thank the clients for their attendance and enclose marketing brochures with your firm's services.

Part Three   Reading Task

Reading Task One

Possible answer:

✓ As a Chinese, Lin Kai's self-abasement over the dinner is a sign of modesty and respect. But Anson, from a culture that gives efficiency and work a high priority, may take it as a sincere remark. So he thinks Lin Kai really thinks that such a big dinner is nothing and Lin Kai doesn't think the spending on such a dinner is very much. How can he be taken as an economical and bright business partner?

✓ Lin Kai's meaning: I said that in this way just to show my modesty and respect to you, as we always say so in this case. I hope you fully take my respect.

✓ Anson's meaning: Even such a big dinner is nothing to him. No doubt, he would spend much more money on food that would be left over a lot. It is a waste. He is not careful with money. We can't invest into a company managed by such a person.

✓ As to this situation, my suggestion is: First, make sure that Anson understands that this big dinner is arranged for him specially, and it is Lin Kai's privilege to serve him well. Secondly, try to show the company's strong points and its strong wish to be invested by the German company.

✓ Now we can see in interaction, a good wish doesn't always lead to a good result. In cross-culture business communication, we should know about the different values, different observations and customs of our counterparts and try to monitor the social situation in a way we expect or are oriented.

Reading Task Two

    1-3: ACD

Part Five Assignment

| 咸鴨蛋 | salted duck eggs | 皮蛋 | preserved eggs |

煎蛋　fried eggs　　　　　　　　　脆皮乳鴿　crispy pigeon

皮蛋豆腐　tofu with preserved eggs

臘肉炒香芹　sautéed preserved pork with celery

青椒肉絲　shredded pork with green pepper

豉汁蒸排骨　steamed spareribs in black bean sauce

牛肉炖土豆　braised beef with potatoes

韭菜炒雞蛋　scrambled egg with leek

紅燒甲魚　braised turtle in brown sauce

香辣蟹　sautéed crab in hot spicy sauce

Unit Eleven Marketing & Sales

Part One Listening Task

Listening Task One

    There are two ways of getting as much as possible about potential customers and possible competition from other companies when we set out to market a new product. The first is through primary research and this (1) <u>involves</u> getting out there and talking to people. We prepare a questionnaire that considers the likes, dislikes, and (2) <u>income levels</u> of consumers, and we try to find out what newspapers and (3) <u>magazines</u> they read. This information can also be gathered (4) via a phone interview. We can also make note of what shoppers buy when they go out as well as using television panels where consumers and retailers give (5) feedback. The other type of research requires (6) less physical effort and is often referred to as (7) secondary research. Sales reports and trade figures are (8) analyzed for existing information. Magazines, newspapers, and government (9) publications as well as Internet searches provide useful data. So let's consider some of these in more (10) detail.

Tape Script

Speaker:

  Good morning, everyone. Well, I think we are all clear by now about the importance of knowing as much as possible about potential customers and possible competition from other companies when we set out to market a new product. Today, I want to look at the different ways we collect data. We want to find out all we can about consumers' income, likes, dislikes, and where they live. We also need to investigate our competitors' prices and methods of advertising.

  There are two ways of getting this information. The first is through primary research and this involves getting out there and talking to people. We prepare a questionnaire that considers the likes, dislikes, and income levels of consumers, and we try to find out what newspapers and magazines they read. This information can also be gathered via a phone interview. We can also make note of what shoppers buy when they go out as well as using television panels where consumers and retailers give feedback.

  The other type of research requires less physical effort and is often referred to as secondary research. Sales reports and trade figures are analyzed for existing information. Magazines, newspapers, and government publications as well as Internet searches provide useful data. So let's consider some of these in more detail …

Listening Task Two

  (√) 1. Pick up on a person's personality traits.

  (×) 2. When extremely busy, make an automated answering machine get your phone calls.

(√) 3. Create an emotional link with the customer.

(×) 4. Deal with complaints head on.

(√) 5. Recognize indecisiveness and help customers make a decision.

(√) 6. Like people and recognize their needs and wants.

(×) 7. Show customers what they are asking for.

(√) 8. Be a good listener.

(√) 9. Sell products that you like.

(×) 10. The word 「try」 should not be in a good sales person's vocabulary.

Tape Script

Speaker:

In the traditional approach to selling, the salesman was someone who did it because he couldn't find another job. Selling often meant sticking your foot in the front door, bullying your way into a home, or conning the person into coughing up for a product that they may or may not need like a set of encyclopedias for the children. These days the image of the salesperson has changed drastically and a lot of preparation and psychology have gone into turning out a good salesperson. Still it does help if you have certain personality characteristics before you start. A person who's able to quickly pick up on the personality traits of another and build on this insight to create an emotional link is likely to succeed at sales. Such a salesperson recognizes the indecisiveness of a prospective customer and helps them make up their mind in favor of the product. It's important that the salesperson likes people and is able to tune into their different needs and wants. It's also important to be a good listener and pay attention to the value system of the customer. It's also a good idea to sell products that interest you as this makes selling easier.

Part Two Speaking Task

2. 1) b   2) c   3) d   4) e   5) h   6) g   7) f   8) a

Part Three　Reading Task

Reading Task One

（F）1. Four marketing strategies are mentioned in the passage in order to realize the company goals.

（T）2. Via price reduction strategy, it's possible for the company to capture greater share of market.

（F）3. Both price reduction strategy and production differentiation strategy require raising product prices to increase profit margins.

（T）4. Market segmentation divides the whole market into several smaller ones according to the characteristics of customers' behavior.

（T）5. The marketing programs carried out by companies should cater to the needs and preferences of the individual segments.

Reading Task Two

1-5: BDCCD

Unit Twelve　Financial Matters

Part One　Listening Task

Listening Task One

Fixed Assets	
Buildings	400,000
Equipment	50,000
Motor Vehicles	60,000
Total	510,000

Current Assets	
Stock	7,000
Cash	2,000
Trade debtor	5,000
Total	14,000
Current Liabilities	
Bank overdraft	2,500
Trade creditors	800
Total	3,300

Tape Script

Finance Director:

The company's fixed assets consist of buildings worth 400,000 dollars, various types of equipment with a total value of 50,000 dollars, and motor vehicles that are worth 60,000 dollars.

Our current assets include stock worth 7,000 dollars plus 2,000 dollars in cash. We are also owed 5,000 dollars by various debtors.

As for current liabilities, we still have an overdraft of 2,500 dollars and we owe 800 dollars to various creditors.

Listening Task Two

Advantages:

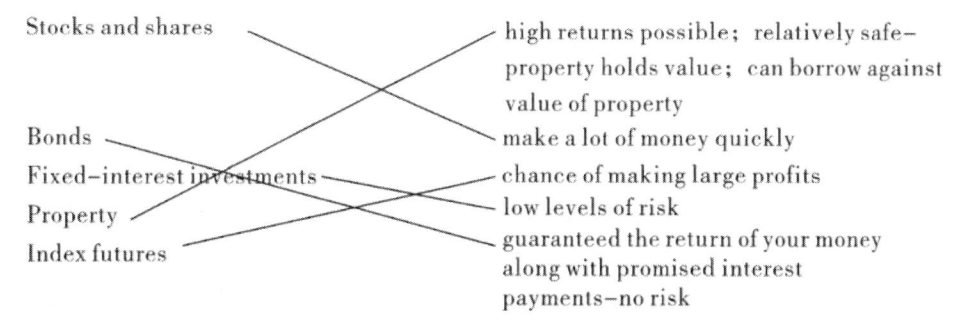

- Stocks and shares — chance of making large profits
- Bonds — guaranteed the return of your money along with promised interest payments—no risk
- Fixed-interest investments — low levels of risk
- Property — high returns possible; relatively safe—property holds value; can borrow against value of property
- Index futures — make a lot of money quickly

Disadvantages:

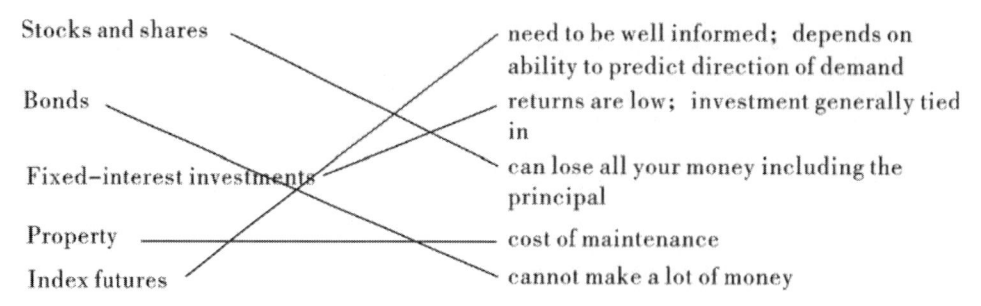

Stocks and shares — need to be well informed; depends on ability to predict direction of demand

Bonds — returns are low; investment generally tied in

Fixed-interest investments — can lose all your money including the principal

Property — cost of maintenance

Index futures — cannot make a lot of money

(matching: Stocks and shares → can lose all your money including the principal; Bonds → returns are low; investment generally tied in; Fixed-interest investments → cannot make a lot of money; Property → cost of maintenance; Index futures → need to be well informed; depends on ability to predict direction of demand)

Tape Script

Investor: So, what can you tell me about the different options for investing my money?

Expert: Well, there are a number of things you can do. Let's start with stocks and shares. The obvious advantage here is that you can make a lot of money quickly. But on the down side, you can lose all your money, including the principal. It can be risky.

Investor: I see. What about a more low-risk investment?

Expert: Okay. Well, there are a couple of options here. You can invest in bonds. With bonds, you are guaranteed the return of your money along with promised interest payments. There is no risk. Of course, the disadvantage is that the returns are not very high. The same is true with other fixed interest investments. As with bonds, there are low levels of risks and guaranteed returns on your investment. But the returns are low and, generally, your investment is tied in for a fixed period of time.

Investor: What about property? Is that a good thing to invest my money in?

Expert: It can be. With property, there is the possibility of high returns. And it is relatively safe investment as property generally holds its value. And you can borrow against the value of the property. One drawback is that you may have to spend money on the maintenance of the property. Its sale value will depend on its location and on the property market at the time of the sale.

Investor: I've heard of something called 「index futures」. What can you tell me about them?

Expert: Ah, yes. Well, here there is the possibility of making large profits if prices move in the direction that you anticipated. Of course, you need to be well informed. Success depends on your ability to predict the direction of demand.

Part Three Reading Task

Reading Task One

　　(F) 1. The Itsbuzzin company started up with $380 million.

　　(T) 2. Market analysis for online fashion wear sales was not realistic.

　　(T) 3. Itsbuzzin's high operating costs were one of the major causes of its failure.

　　(F) 4. Advertisers, shareholders and staff were compensated for their losses.

　　(F) 5. Staff spoke different languages so there were large expense accounts.

　　(T) 6. Offering free delivery turned out to be a very expensive decision.

Reading Task Two

　　1-3: CAD

國家圖書館出版品預行編目(CIP)資料

實用職場英語教程 / 石轉轉 主編. -- 第一版.
-- 臺北市：崧博出版：崧燁文化發行, 2018.09
　面；　公分
ISBN 978-957-735-504-1(平裝)
1.英語 2.職場 3.讀本
805.18　　　　107015392

書　名：實用職場英語教程
作　者：石轉轉 主編
發行人：黃振庭
出版者：崧博出版事業有限公司
發行者：崧燁文化事業有限公司
E-mail：sonbookservice@gmail.com
粉絲頁　　　　　網　址
地　址：台北市中正區重慶南路一段六十一號八樓815室
8F.-815, No.61, Sec. 1, Chongqing S. Rd., Zhongzheng Dist., Taipei City 100, Taiwan (R.O.C.)
電　話：(02)2370-3310　傳　真：(02) 2370-3210
總經銷：紅螞蟻圖書有限公司
地　址：台北市內湖區舊宗路二段 121 巷 19 號
電　話：02-2795-3656　傳真：02-2795-4100　網址：
印　刷：京峯彩色印刷有限公司（京峰數位）

本書版權為西南財經大學出版社所有授權崧博出版事業有限公司獨家發行電子書繁體字版。若有其他相關權利及授權需求請與本公司聯繫。

定價：350 元
發行日期：2018 年 9 月第一版
◎ 本書以POD印製發行